Treats

Treats

A collection of short stories

Lara Williams

FREIGHT BOOKS

First published in the UK 2016

Freight Books
49–53 Virginia Street
Glasgow, G1 1TS
www.freightbooks.co.uk

A CIP catalogue reference for this book is available from the British Library.

ISBN 978-1-910449-70-7
eISBN 978-1-910449-71-4

Typeset by Freight in Plantin & Aktiv Grotesk
Printed and bound by Bell and Bain, Glasgow

the publisher acknowledges investment from
Creative Scotland toward the publication of this book

Lara Williams is a writer based in Manchester. She has had short fiction published by *McSweeney's*, *Litro* and various other publications and websites, and her journalism and non-fiction has appeared in the *Guardian*, *NME* and the *Manchester Evening News*.

For my lovely family.

Contents

It Begins

And so it begins. You graduate university. You move back home, slotting neatly into your single bed, examining the tears in the wallpaper, the posters on the wall. You sleep in till eleven. Your mum cooks you porridge, setting it down on the kitchen table, the mealy textures of your childhood. 'I've got a good feeling about this one,' she says. 'You were born to work in an art gallery.'

You wait your turn. The room smells dusty and grand. You notice a single oat clinging to the hem of your skirt. You flick it off and it leaves behind a tiny, white "O". O dear, you think. O no. You are annoyed at your mum for having made you porridge. You want to call her. If you think I am an adult, you want to say, then why are you making me meals consisting primarily of milk? A man in a black shirt with a clipboard and a walkie-talkie calls your name. You take a seat. You say you are skilled in research, you completed your dissertation on contemporary art and twentieth century literature, you have customer service experience, you are an avid gallery goer. 'Fantastic,' he says. 'Great.'

'Are you aware this is not a paid position?'

You sit in front of the television stroking the cat. You are wearing pyjamas. You cannot believe you are a person who has had sex, who has driven a car. The cat massages its claws into you, it dispenses a steady purr. You go to the kitchen and make yourself a slice of toast and a gin and tonic.

You get an office job. You assimilate with business graduates, with their hearty sense of cynicism, a premature world-weariness, worn like a badge of honour. So pleased with their early resignation, their: this, this is life. This marching course of spreadsheets and workflows and thin-lipped jokes in strategising brainstorms, this is all there is and we knew all along, while you were dilly-dallying with your Chaucer, frolicking with your intertextuality, we were squirreling away the capacity to deal with this. Imagine being that lacking in idealism, you think. Imagine being that lacking in wonder, aspiring to jobs in logistics or IT services, imagine never entertaining frothy careers scouting bands, imagine never picturing yourself in front of a glossy iMac. Did it make the heartbreak easier or earlier? You grip your rosy ideals, your soppy security blanket.

And then you meet him. He has wintry eyes, a handsome voice and he wears smart suits. He is older than you. He shows you how to make the battery life on your phone last longer by switching off the Wi-Fi. He knows stuff like that. You love everything he says. You want to write it down, to run your fingers over it, to hold it up to your face and kiss it. You think about his heart a lot, his kind heart. You imagine it a sinewy, sloppy substance, like a thick broth. You imagine it in your hands. You hold your ear to his chest to hear it beating and you don't ever let yourself think about the day when it will stop. One day you tell him this is just a stopgap, just until you figure out what you're supposed to do. He places three fingers in the spaces between your knuckles and you feel a contentment quite close to death. Before you know it you wear sensible shoes to middle management meetings and caveat proposed website frameworks before clip-clopping home to get dinner on.

You are walking through airport security, clutching your passport. You feel like two children on an adventure. You spritz yourself with perfume in Duty Free while he browses digital cameras. This is it, you think. This is happening. He asks you on the last night of your holiday. You say yes straight away. It might as well have been written down on a piece of paper, folded in your pocket all along. You guessed the correct answer! You win a life together!

You are lying on the floor wearing a red hooded sweatshirt and grey tracksuit bottoms. You hear the front door open. 'I'm not well,' you say, 'I feel sick, I think I'm dying.' He drops his briefcase, wraps his arms around your waist and throws you over his shoulder. You feel giddy and light, like a fluttering, translucent piece of paper. 'Do you feel less sick now?' he asks, spinning you around the room. 'How about now?' You giggle and squeak, thinking: why is he back from work early?

You are drinking tea in bed. He sits on the edge of the mattress wearing his wool coat. He holds his palm to your cheek. It is cold and you flinch away. 'Helen in Finance says her husband is looking for a Marketing Manager so I've forwarded her your CV,' he says. 'Maybe you should post out the portfolios you put together?' You take a long gulp of tea and stare straight ahead. 'Okay,' he says. 'Okay. I can post them out.' He kisses your knee beneath the duvet. As he leaves the room you notice his eyes. They look tired.

He comes home late. You have fallen asleep on the settee. You open your eyes, your face feels mulched. You struggle to sit up. You think maybe you're still sleeping. 'After work drinks?' you ask. 'Was she there?' You hadn't intended to sound so vitriolic. 'If you're so convinced I'm fucking her,' he replies. 'Then maybe I just should.'

You sit across from him in a hammy Italian bistro, winding spaghetti around your fork between sips of white wine. You look at him and his face is old and unfamiliar. Who are you? you think. And why are you touching my hand?

You are in a pale green room with floor-to-ceiling windows. You are sitting cross-legged. You catch the eye of a man you haven't seen before. He is attractive. He has dark eyes and you hold his gaze. The instructor counts your breathing: In...two... three...four... Out...two...three...four... As you collect your coat he touches your shoulder. 'I don't normally do this,' he says. 'But would you like to go for a drink?' You sit next to him and when his leg rests against yours you let it. It's late and you're drunk. 'Let's get out of here,' you say. You fall over and he catches you, holding your face and pressing his lips to yours. You respond. It is that easy, you think. It is already done. You tell him you're married. 'I know,' he replies. 'So what.' You hail a taxi. You're not sure if the fall was deliberate. You never see him again.

At some point it occurs to you: you will divorce. Divorce is our destiny.

He is packing his bags and you are hysterical. 'It doesn't matter what her name is,' he tells you. 'It doesn't matter who she is.' You go downstairs and find a knife in the kitchen, scraping the thin blade across your wrist. Well I suppose it doesn't matter if I open up my veins, you think. I suppose it doesn't matter if I bleed out right here on this floor. The door slams behind him.

You cry and sleep, a routine of sorts, performed several times daily. And yet you worry that maybe you're not quite feeling it fully, that it hasn't quite reached the tips of your fingers, lying dormant under a few layers of skin, when suddenly it shoots out, pouring forth from every orifice, spinning circles around the room and it is all there is.

It is all there is.

You are now one of them. You have joined that special club and your initiation rites are a series of squeezed shoulders, of weak smiles. Stories of former breakups, bad boyfriends, husbands cheating, confessionals offered up, little titbits of consolation, like treats. Fuck you, you think. Fuck you, this is different. This is different because this is happening to me. Your friends want you to talk about it but you cannot. 'There is no vocabulary for heartbreak,' you say. 'There is no point.'

You take up painting. There is something pleasingly definite about it, slicking fat strips of colour onto a canvas. You think about how strange it is to still have absolutes like this, like marriage, in this day and age. Couldn't there be another option, leasing it out for five, maybe ten years then reviewing it when the time comes. We are a generation of renters not buyers. Your friend Suze tells you to stop being cynical.

You have a date. You wear a tailored, chiffon dress and a simple white gold pendant. He is prompt, polite, he pulls your chair out for you and asks you what you would like to drink. You tilt your head back and hold the menu in front of you. He rolls up his sleeves revealing thick, hairy arms. You ask him what he does and he says he works in capital projects. You ask him if he enjoys it and he says it pays the bills. A tall blonde woman walks by and his eyes follow her past the table, past the bar, through the swinging doors and into the toilets. You wish someone had warned you about tall blonde women earlier. Sexually transmitted diseases, drink driving, bar snacks and tall blonde women. The real stranger danger. Your food arrives and you feel an anxiety about eating you have not felt in years. He says he's glad you ordered a salad, a woman should watch her weight. He says he likes your dress and he's looking forward to taking it off later. He says it's good that you're doing so well in your career, just so long as you don't turn into a bitch, like his boss, now there's a woman who wants it. I don't have to listen to this shit, you think, and at once, you realise you don't have to. You dab French dressing from your mouth and set the napkin on the table. 'I'm terribly sorry,' you say. 'But I have somewhere I have to be.'

You are gardening. You look at your hands as you pull knots of weeds from the dirt. You have a young woman's hands with tapered, elegant fingers and small, square fingernails. The sun falls warmly on your face. It is nearly time for lunch.

A Lover's Guide To Meeting Shy Girls; Or; Break Up Record

It was not so much that Devon's heart had been broken, that seemed too cavalier a vernacular, too vague a phrase; his experience had been more precise, more surgical, he felt. Prised from beneath his rib cage, removed carefully (and perhaps even lovingly?) then slowly, studiously, crushed. It came as quite the surprise.

He had believed with all the necessary vanity he was the charmer, the heartbreaker. What's more he recognised a certain responsibility, a certain culpability, selecting his words, monitoring his actions, mindful of the capacity they had to flatter a young lady, to write cheques that for reasons he didn't need to explain he could not cash.

The heartbreaker, it transpired, was Emily; a very unlikely candidate. Emily was a sweet girl, a shy thing really, benign as a piece of fruit. She had a fundamental softness to her; a feathery way of talking, a lightness and delicacy in everything she said or did. He remembered their first date. He had taken her to a French patisserie, ordering a tray of macarons and a bottle of Champagne because that is, as everyone knows, how you romance shy girls. With French things and cake. She chose a pale pink macaron, with a chocolate ganache, tentatively biting into it. He looked on, surprised it was the pastry that crumbled beneath her bite, and not her lips and teeth against the meringue.

There was something about her softness that made him feel more viscerally himself. More potent in her presence. A serious and scholarly grey against her faded pastels. What's more, she was a dancer. And he, well, he was a musician. How could it have gone so horribly wrong?

They were watching Annie Hall, on a Saturday morning,

her laptop balanced on the floral coastline of her duvet, her blonde hair spilling around her face. 'I don't think we should be a couple anymore,' she said, gazing off to the side of the room, staring at the antique typewriter she used to hang her necklaces, her ballet pumps tied to the door, adding: 'Doesn't Woody Allen have very brown eyes?' Ha Ha Ha! he thought, you silly, whimsical thing; you stupid, flighty bitch. Ha Ha Ha! But then she got out of bed, pulled a grey hoodie over her satin nightgown, and wouldn't stop crying until he had left.

And so, he decided to write a breakup record. A scooped out Kübler-Ross road trip across the pitted landscape of his grief; spectral strings, whispered vocals, maudlin hand claps, even a bit of tambourine. It felt a fitting tribute. An appropriate exorcism. The one thing that might serve to cleanse his soul.

But that was seven years ago and with each passing day the album was not complete, it became more important for him to make a perfect record. To make THE perfect record. The perfect breakup record.

He was learning Ableton.

Morag, his new girlfriend, did not care for music. But more than that, she couldn't understand why he was still writing an album about a girl he had not seen in seven years; a girl, that in effect, he had only been in a relationship with for a little over four months.

Morag had recently taken to eating raw beetroot, chopped into cubes, served without any seasoning or dressing. She would sit cross-legged in front of the television, watching cooking shows, watching dating shows, and sometimes, watching cooking and dating shows. She would laugh. She would laugh a cruel, unforgiving laugh.

'We got that wrong,' she said, pointing at the screen. 'We got food wrong. We got sex wrong. We're the generation that got a lot of stuff wrong.'

She looked round at him, beetroot juice smeared across her mouth and fingers, like a recently devoured kill. He blinked back at her, squinting into the opaque universe of her thoughts.

'I'm going to work on my record,' he said, making for the basement.

When he and Emily first split up he imagined his longing for her a pulled piece of chewing gum, thinning with time, gently breaking and falling balletically apart. But what he found was, over time, it got worse; and with each passing day, passing moment, it became increasingly impossible to articulate into music the pain of having lost her, at having lost such a sweet, shy girl.

Sometimes Morag would be sweet; or try to be sweet, but it always felt performative, an artifice of sweetness, aspartame smiles and candied gestures she could never quite pull off. They would lock eyes, momentarily complicit in their theatre, and she would drop the act, shouting at him for not having done the washing up, swearing, or doing something else similarly uncouth.

He would catch himself mid-outlandish gesture. One time they were walking through the park and he grabbed her face, pressed his mouth to her ear, and made some strange animal sound, some howling yelp, because he didn't know what else to say. He had not felt like this with Emily; his feelings for her were certain, assured, a thick unyielding presence at the centre of his chest. His feelings for Morag were not certain, terrifying and vertiginous, hazy as a waltz.

He tinkered at his laptop, playing with different samples, dropping in different beats. He wrote and rewrote the lyrics. He slowed down his vocals eight hundred percent, stretching them out so they felt drowsy and desultory, as static and fractured as the tide. But nothing was good. Nothing was ever good enough. Eventually he gave up, returning upstairs to join Morag in front of the television.

He sat on the floor beside her. 'Nothing's working,' he said. 'Nothing I make sounds right.'

She rolled her eyes, biting a cube of beetroot, offering him a piece. 'You'll get over it,' she said.

He ate it from her hand and leaned his head against her shoulder; breathing in the sweet sweat smell of her jumper, the bobbles tickling his nose.

'What if I don't?' he said. 'What if I don't ever get over it?'

She shrugged his head from her shoulder and turned to look at him. 'You will,' she said, her brown eyes extending into his, like gentle tiny hands.

One Of Those Life Things

You thought you might have exited your twenties, before announcing in whisky hushed tones, a ribbon-y flick of your wrist, that you had been left for some kid in their twenties, some baby, some blonde piece. You feel like some version of yourself sent from a future, dark timeline, all feather boas and fingernails. He hadn't even the decency to have done it at a point when you could have properly committed to the role. Your options scatter like playing cards in front of you, offering only wishy-washy monologue, half-assed character pieces. Where does one go from here? Aerobics and amdram? Pilates and prozac? Bridge and bourbon? What is the narrative here?

You look for an apartment. Somewhere high up and central, somewhere you can flesh out and possess; your dim light bloating through like a Halloween pumpkin. A houseshare is out of the question. You sit on the living room floor, dividing your stuff into piles, His 'n' Hers, mournfully compartmentalised into past, present and future; present the buffer zone between, a veritable no-man's land, ripe for the taking. You both have eyes on the garlic crusher. A bitten, crochet throw, a housewarming gift from your aunt, sags sadly unclaimed. The curtains heave against the breeze of a half-opened window, taking steady breaths; the house has grown tolerant to your bickering, indifferent to your swipes; it rolls its eyes and shrugs its shoulders. You used to lie in bed, listening to its creaks and moans, the boiler chugging off and on, thinking you did still like his smell, you were still very much in favour of his smell. Your best friend Kitty scowls dutifully, scowling like a pro. He remains upstairs, appearing only occasionally, offering to help with the heavy stuff, then returning upstairs. There is no goodbye. There is no need.

You remember how he'd fuss in the kitchen, asking if there was anything you wanted to watch on television. 'I am bored,' you would reply. 'I am b o r e d.'

Kitty drops her cigarette on the living room floor, stamping it out with a canary yellow boot. 'Good riddance,' she yells. 'Good riddance to bad rubbish.' You slam the door and go straight to the shop to buy wine.

Your new apartment is located in the university district off Oxford Road; potted between 24 hour convenience and grimly lit takeaways. You swipe two mirrors from the street, grubby but intact, and a pretty wooden box, marvelling at your own resourcefulness. Who'd let a ticket like this slip through their fingers? Who'd let a number like this get away?

'Well, exactly,' Kitty says, while you stack copies of Vogue in the corner, balancing the television on top, vine fairylights around the window. It looks good. It looks like a single girl's apartment. Kitty recognises a framed John Coltrane photograph as a birthday present from him.

'Oh no!' she says. 'There are to be no traces of He. He must be white-washed. He must be erased from the history books like the atrocity He is.'

She drops it into a bin liner. The glass cracks. You survey the flat, the threaded scatter cushions across the bed, the Toulouse-Lautrec pictures on the walls. You look upon your new manageable life like a Polly Pocket in the palm of your hand. After Kitty leaves you fall fully clothed to sleep.

It is at night that you hear the screams.

A disembodied howl tears through the flat ripping you from your sleep. You jump wild to the window to locate the source, peering into the thin avenue, but you cannot see anything or anyone. You stare at the blank pavement, lit in orange circles, the breeze trailing the occasional plastic bag or dried leaf into the road. You wait there a while, the screams echoing and reverberating around your flat. You think about calling the police. You hold your phone in your hand, poised at the window, before going back to bed, waking to the hollow quiet of morning.

You skip your period. It makes sense. You have been eating less, beginning only to feed, handfuls of cereal, snatches of bread, meals now seem a pointless ceremony. Food has lost its flavour, only its texture can be noted. Your menstrual cycle has grown dopey. Wha? Today? It slipped my mind! You are, if anything, grateful for the reprieve, one month off in two hundred and twenty eight, it seems only fair, heck, it seems like basic common sense. You skip another. You sense the familiar twinges, the usual reminders, snapping twice at strangers, waking crying from a dream, and yet nothing, not a drop. You study the lining of your underwear like a forensic scientist. Hopeful ventures to the toilet result only in disappointment. Oh well, you think. Administrative error. Probably brought on by stress. Last Tuesday you padded around in your pyjamas, sipping a sallow cup of tea, when it occurred to you that you should be at work, as you should every Tuesday, every weekday in fact.

'You can take a little time off?' your boss cooed. 'If you think that would help.'

Can you not cut the same slack to your reproductive faculties? Can you not afford this base level of human compassion to your own body? What are you, a monster? The third skipped period is the clincher.

'For chrissake,' Kitty says. 'I wish I could pee on that goddamned stick for you.'

She seats you with a bowl of iced tea like summer punch; slices of lemon bob hopefully in the water, the ice nudges sweetly against the glass. You scoop a cup with both hands as if receiving communion, a last ditch attempt with him upstairs – are you seeing this, fella? This one's for you! – before retiring to the bathroom where Kitty has lit candles and left the test half-opened and to the side, the peculiar romance of friendship, and you sit, staring at your smugly unsoiled underwear, and pee on the goddamned stick. It is, of course, positive; which seems a bloody presumptuous lexicography.

'What are you going to do?' Kitty says.

You are reading lines from *Just Seventeen*. You are a freeze-frame from *Jackie*. You look at your shoes, flower print plimsolls worn thin at the heel, with soiled smudged laces pulled tight in a bow. How long have you had these shoes? Three, maybe four, years? Why don't you have nicer shoes? Why don't you wear heels? Kitty paces around the apartment, her hand held navally to her brow. She sits down, wrapping both arms around you, pinning your elbows to your waist, and squeezes.

'Well obviously I am not going to have it,' you say. 'I mean, obviously.'

Kitty offers to spend the night, to rent a movie, to cook you dinner, but you tell her you are fine.

'I'm fine,' you say, noticing you are cupping your stomach, ever so gently, in your hand.

You cannot sleep. The screams make it impossible. You throw back the covers and observe your body. It has become something else; something smooth and mechanical, something fit-for-purpose. We are all animals, you think. We are all animals and we are pretending not to be. A thought occurs to you, coiled and distant, looped in another universe, as secret as incest. What if you keep it? You dream of his sleeping back, his navy t-shirt creamy against the dark, before you are woken by a scream, forgetting momentarily where you are.

'I'm pregnant,' you tell your GP. 'And essentially I need not to be.'

The GP types something into his computer. Pregnant + Needs Not To Be = Abortion? 'You are twenty-nine,' he says.

'Yes, I am aware of that,' you reply.

'Lots of women have babies when they're twenty-nine. Twenty-nine is a good age to have a baby,' he says.

'I am also aware of that,' you reply.

'Why?' he asks, as you smooth your skirt, a demonstrative gesture of dignity, drumming your fingernails against the table, kicking your heel to the floor.

'My career,' you reply, as he types something, once more, into his computer; assumedly checking the box that says One Of Them.

Outside you light a cigarette. Smoking has taken a new gravity, a fresh poignancy, and you relish each inhalation, blowing thick plumes into the sky. You pluck your phone from your pocket. 'Would you like to go for a coffee?' you type. You finish your cigarette. 'In hell,' you add, flicking it to the ground.

'I watched *The Shining* last night,' you tell Kitty. 'Shelley Duvall is a woman I can relate to.' Kitty rolls her eyes.

'Because she is a bad actress?' she replies. 'Or because she is a really bad actress?' She leans over gloating at the bartender.

'He keeps looking at you,' she says. 'Why don't you go and say hello?' You glance furtively across; he is tall, broad, with sleepy eyes and a jaw like a science project.

'Because it's a swiz,' you say. 'It's a horrible scrap that I don't want any part of.'

She sighs and finishes her drink.

'Plus, I am carrying another man's child.'

You giggle. You giggle in an absent, hysterical way, that doesn't feel attached or a part of you; silly trills peeping from your lips, fluttering nervously in the air. You can't stop. 'You know all of her hair fell out?' you say.

'What?' Kitty replies.

'Shelley Duvall. All of her hair fell out while she was filming.' You wind a lock of hair around your finger. You giggle again. 'It just fell out,' you say. 'Poof.'

Kitty studies the cocktail menu and orders another round of drinks. 'This is nice,' she says. 'This is like the old days.'

You lie tipsy in bed, a cool whip of sheet curls over your leg, you press your face into the pillow. You listen to your heart beating into the mattress; its stoic, earthy thump, jingoistic in its resolve, foolhardy in its rhythm. You lift yourself out of bed, taking a glass of water to the window, shouts and screams rising from below. How are you expected to sleep with this? How is anyone? You Google foetal development on your phone, swiping through the pictures, a grotesque slideshow that slips over your eyes like butter. You sense some metaphorical mountain, some veering, husked peak, feeling not that you have started to climb it, but that you are still stood blinking dumbly at its foot, unable to believe it is even there at all. 'I need to talk to you,' you type into your phone. The screams swell and bounce around your flat. 'In hell,' you add, pressing send.

Kitty pulls up in front of your building as you stand waiting outside knapsack in hand; book, iPad and sanitary towels, ladies need their trinkets.

'Hop in sugar,' she says, pushing open the door. She is wearing candy pink sunglasses and a single plait pinned neatly across her brow. 'What do you want to listen to?' she asks. 'Now That's What I Call Jazz or Maybe Baby: The Best of Buddy Holly?' She holds the plastic covers in front of her face, your glossed reflection, watery and slanted, frowns back at you.

'Radio,' you reply. 'Talk radio.'

'She's here for her rhinoplasty,' Kitty tells the receptionist, and he forces a smile, recognising the joke for the kindness it is. 'Look at this idiot,' Kitty says, wafting the tissue-y paper of some gossip rag, some tanned blonde, grinning in a bikini, a title purring, 'How I lost the baby weight without even trying.' Kitty is a good friend. You wear a hospital gown and it chafes against your legs.

'Correct me if I'm wrong,' you say, popping your hip, sweeping your hair over your shoulder. 'But is this Marant

Autumn/Winter?'

The anaesthetist makes his rounds; he is distant, rehearsed, with the saintly vernacular of science. What's worse, is that he is handsome, and you, you are strung out and braless, up the houses, though soon not to be. The gynaecologist follows, short and stocky, her cat eye glasses balanced lopsidedly on her nose. She is tired; she has an underactive thyroid and a cat with leukaemia.

'Stripper glasses,' Kitty whispers. 'Female doctors are always wearing stripper glasses.' A nurse calls your name.

'It is nearly time,' she says, pulling up a wheelchair.

You suddenly panic, scooping the soft pouch of your stomach in your hand, this last trace of him set to be ripped out and at your own request. You look at Kitty. She grapples for words like confetti in the breeze. There are no words. There are no words for this basic animal trauma.

'It is one of those life things,' she whispers, hurriedly. 'It is just one of those life things.'

As you are pushed through the double doors, you think suddenly of your mother, wearing a wide-brimmed hat, slopping you in sun cream every day of summer, no matter how warm or cool the weather. How she would cover you and forget to cover herself; her skin sizzling to flakes.

'You know we talked about having a baby,' you say to the nurse. 'Just once. But we did talk about it.'

The nurse kicks on the breaks. 'Huh?' she says.

You wake up returned to your hospital bed, achy and disoriented, groggy and without words. It is done, over; zapped like a nuisance fly.

'My nose is blocked,' you tell the nurse who hovers at your side.

'That happens sometimes,' she says, handing you a tissue.

You press it to your face, blowing into it inelegantly; a mess of spit, tears and mucus. You can't imagine anybody in the world is more disgusting than you are right now. Kitty places her hand on top of your own.

'Can I get you anything?' she says. You think, you would very much like some ice-cream. You think you would like to be left alone. You think, really, you would very much like some ice-cream. Miles Davis, *Blue in Green*, plays on some distant radio; and it feels like it is raining, everywhere, inside.

Kitty drives you home, clutching your elbow as she walks you to your door, though you can manage perfectly well on your own.

'I'd really rather stay,' she says, holding your arm.

You tell her you just want to sleep, agreeing to let her go to the shops, to buy you some pistachio Häagen-Dazs, and leave it at that. She returns with three cartons, removing a bowl and spoon from the kitchen, scooping the ice-cream into pale green baubles. You allow her the gesture. 'You call me,' she says.

'You call me if you need anything.' You fall asleep watching the news.

You awake on the settee, in the early hours of the morning, erased and numb, huffing yourself to your bed. Your stomach is puffed and swollen, too sore for the elastic waist of your pyjamas, which you have to roll down, exposing its rosy globe. You stare at your lumpen form; a throbbing mass, an object of pain. The shouts and screams, the usual cacophony, prove too insufferable an additional discomfort, and with sudden resolve, you pick up your phone and call the police.

'I'd like to report some screaming,' you say. 'I'd like to report some very loud, very present, screaming.'

You give your address; meticulously intoning the letters and numbers of your postcode. You hear the faint peck of a tapped keyboard.

'Is that the university district?' the operator asks.

'It is,' you reply.

'It's just students,' she says. 'It's just students making a racket.'

You pull back your curtains, peering outside, funnelling the howls that fill your room. You start to cry, just a little, just a bit; your doughy fat middle jiggling in the pale blue dark. You want only for him to be there, to hold you, in the most stupid, most childlike way.

'But you don't understand,' you say. 'I hear screams constantly. I hear screams all through the night.'

'It is hell,' you say. 'It is like living in hell.'

You stare into the street, the jagged caterwaul of the road, the oppressive palmistry of the pavement.

'Well if you don't want to live in hell,' the operator replies, as clear as sunrise, as bald as earth, 'then I suggest you move.'

Both Boys

She met both boys on the same night. The brown haired boy and the blonde haired one. Both of them in one night. She couldn't believe her luck.

The brown haired boy said he wanted to charm her. To take her out dancing and buy her potted plants. To knock her off her feet.

The blonde one placed his palm flat beneath the waistline of her jeans. He told her she must have been put on the planet for his express delectation. He said he felt he deserved a girl – a nice girl like her – and why didn't she join him in the bathroom; navigating her away like she was something he already owned. But that's blondes for you. And with all that gold framing their peripheries it's little wonder.

She had sex with them both, on the same night too; because she was amongst many things, an equal opportunist. She had sex with the brown haired boy first. He told her she was very beautiful and came with a muted panic. She'd spotted him across the crowded kitchen thinking he looked polite or nice.

She had sex with the blonde boy some two hours later. By that point she was in the mood for something more primordial, something more aerobic, something like banging your head into a brick wall. He would not look at her, and when she caught his eye he looked terribly angry, like she had disturbed him working on a very complicated maths equation or doing his taxes. She wriggled out from beneath him and thought: one day you may have a daughter, one day you may well have a daughter.

It turned out they were best friends.

'Best friends?' she said to the blonde haired boy so scornfully she could have spat. 'Best friends in all of the world?'

Lara Williams

'Yes I suppose,' he said; wiping his stomach with her scarf.

'Well if you like each other so much,' she replied. 'Why don't you just get married.'

He buttoned his jeans and fastened his shirt.

'I suppose you want to go out for dinner,' he said. 'I suppose now you want the whole hoopla.'

'No,' she said. 'I don't.' But she did. She did want the whole hoopla. Of course she did.

A week later it was the brown haired boy who asked her on a date. He sent a bunch of flowers, with a tiny card; the paper of which was so fancy she ran her thumb over it for hours. *Allow me to take you out*, it said. *Allow me to take you out on the town!*

She ignored it; ignoring things was a good way of making them disappear.

A week later he sent her an email. *Please excuse the informality of the platform*, it said. *But I should still like to take you out.*

She dragged it to her junk folder, vanishing it away.

He rang her a week after that, calling late at night.

'I hope this isn't because I told you that you were very beautiful,' he said. 'Because I want you to know, I am equally, if not more, curious about your mind.'

She agreed to go out with him. To get it over with.

He sent a car to collect her, travelling her to the outskirts of town. He'd booked a corner table at a French bistro. She couldn't decide on an entrée and so he ordered them all.

'You know,' he said. 'I think we could really make a go of things.' After he walked her to her door he kissed her so tenderly she thought he might cry.

Some days later the blonde haired boy turned up on her doorstep. 'I thought we were going out tonight,' he said, handing her a box of chocolates.

'These are diabetic,' she said. 'Why have you brought me diabetic chocolates?'

'I guess you look diabetic,' he said. 'I think it's your ankles.'

He took her to a pizza place and had terrible table manners. He got very drunk. He spent the whole evening talking about his ex-girlfriend.

'She's the most attractive woman I have ever seen,' he said; and she smiled though the implication made her retreat to some dark inward beyond. He declined to spend the night.

'I have to be up early,' he said. 'Or whatever.'

He told her he would call her. She sat in her living room, watching television, waiting; with the diabetic chocolates in her lap. She savoured every one. Though they essentially tasted like shit, she admired the gesture all the more for its fundamental ineptitude. There was a hollow kindness in ineptitude. There was a sincerity.

But he did not call that night. Or the night after that. Or any of the nights after that. The brown haired boy didn't call either but that was okay; she wasn't at all bothered about him.

Where I Am Supposed To Be

Was the kiss necessary? Did it soften the blow? A pixelated mwah, a chou chou flick of the wrist, a needless pop of the hip. What flavour yoghurt would you like? Peach. Kiss. What time should we meet? Twelve. Kiss. Is it cancer or not cancer? Cancer. Kiss. The kiss felt like a punch to the gut.

I was stood in the kitchen. I was not where I was supposed to be. I moved to the living room, to the bathroom, to the hallway. All were incorrect. Dora padded behind me; Dora the daughter, the flat-footed grace of a toddler. Clea came home and I kissed them both goodbye. I drove to yours catching sight of myself in the mirror. Dark lipstick and brows, like some tweenage flashforward. Blossom has a baby.

I brought chocolate and crisps; we dozed on the sofa watching our reflections in the French windows. You once told me gay women are more likely to put weight on when they're in a relationship. You said stuff like that. I dismissed the idea. Called you homophobic. But now I understood. Women came together and they ate.

'Not compatible with life,' they told you. 'Not bloody compatible with a lot of things,' you'd said. 'Not compatible with my ex-girlfriend. Not compatible with dairy.' We were old. Were we old? We were at that age where people started affixing your age to compliments. Cancer, you said, flicking a stray hair from your arm, is no walk in the cake park. And all deaths end the same.

After, I lay in bed for days. Your absence hanging in the air like a mist. A duvet I couldn't crawl out of. A migraine I couldn't shake. Everything experienced as if underwater. A loose memory forgotten even while it was happening. You were bigger, louder – I'd always been drawn to something more than myself. In size I found certainty, in vitality I was assured. This here is presence. With you gone I felt untethered, wild and drifting, laundry loose on the breeze. I looked in the mirror. My skin was dry and flaking like life was retreating further inside me. My hair had thinned to nervous patches. Grief was messy. It didn't have the elegance of longing, the poetry of heartbreak; its wholeness made it solid, its certainty made it base.

Lying in bed we fought to be tiny. Clea pulled my arms around her, turning over, her back curled against my chest. I'd remove them, drag her around, force her arm over me; two little spoons, negotiating.

I became a murderer, killing things swiftly and effortlessly, killing without even meaning to. The abused come abuser, my turn to get some, dispatching electrical bolts from the tips of my fingers. A decapitating rhetoric that took even me by surprise. Coffee morning with an old friend. Bam! Dead. Running into a colleague at the supermarket. Whallop! Finito.

It balled up, eventually, the loss, sitting inside my body, knotted and out of place like a hot diamond slotted behind my lung. I found myself squinting at my laptop, back to work, my hair damp, my pyjamas freshly washed. I thought: I feel like Helen Hunt, in a movie about Helen Hunt, squinting at her laptop, back to work, her hair damp, her pyjamas freshly washed. Triumph over adversity, life felt like a series of small battles, of smaller wins, twisting and mutating, always, into something else.

For Dora's birthday we had a picnic in the park, the kind we used to have with you. You would bake cake and biscuits. I'd bring sandwiches and tea. Dora spotted a blackbird and wandered off, watching it leap across the grass. 'Come back!' I shouted at her. 'Don't you go off too far!' Girls grew up afraid, you said. I would say things to Dora, treat her in a certain way and you would ask, would I do this differently if she were a boy? The answer, invariably, was yes. I sliced off a piece of cake, bought from the shop. 'Dora,' I called. I wondered if she remembered you at all.

We sat on the sofa, watching an archaeology documentary. They'd dug up a child's skull. It upset Clea to see a child's skull with all its baby teeth still intact. I kissed her forehead. I stroked her hair.

Dora lingered in the hallway like a dream.

'How did they get the skull?' she asked, venturing nearer, her doughy palms tugging at the soft felt of her nightie. I swooped her up, nestling her between us on the sofa, her legs draped limp across mine.

I pressed my nose to her head, inhaling her fleecy ammonia. I felt some wincing, aching pain, slotted behind my lung, dulled as I wrapped both arms around her, and around Clea, holding them close; thinking this week we should all go out and get pizza, thinking I am exactly where I am supposed to be.

This Small Written Thing

When Joseph announced he'd found a job the way one might announce getting TiVo, or getting into Harpo Marx; snaking against the white glow of a rice paper floor lamp, fist on hip, knee crooked jauntily to one side – *Honey, I got the job! The kid stays in the picture! Whatever DID happen to Baby Jane?!* – there was talk of them both moving to London, but it was static, radio interference; what with the renting costs and Flora already working. And so with little argument from either side it was decided he would stay at his brother's in Hammersmith, Monday to Friday, then come home, to Manchester, at the weekend. Though what weekends they could be! – weekends that would extend before them like a single beckoning digit; long, glorious weekends filled with flat whites and breakfast scrambles, languid walks around the art gallery. It was, in many ways, exactly what they needed and they found themselves curiously excited about the separation; planning their evenings apart, their reunions. It could be like the beginning of the relationship again. It could be like dating.

Flora saw him off at the train station; laptop in one hand, small suitcase in the other. He came home the following Friday, arriving into Manchester Piccadilly at quarter past eight, and they went straight out to dinner; wine, penne and candlelight so readily accessible. The next morning they lay in reading the papers, taking it in turns to make coffee. Their flat invited it. It was a homely flat, a sedentary flat, more like a little house than an apartment, porcelain vases erupting dried flowers bound by a constellation of fairy lights, tea lights lit up the peripheries scented like titles for coffee or conceptual art. On Sunday they sampled artisanal cheese, squirreled herbed loaves into canvas satchels at the local farmer's market before returning home to watch a film, entwined on the sofa. Flora dropped him off at the station, his suitcase slightly bigger than the last; on getting back into the car, she noticed he'd left his gloves behind, his hands would be cold, and she felt a pang that wasn't quite pain, more the foreshadow of pain, the blueprint of it.

He got in a little later the next Friday, about ten thirty, and went immediately to bed. 'Sweetheart,' he said, kissing the top of her head. 'I am exhausted.' He spent most of Saturday working, hunched over his computer, looking handsome and dishevelled. As he grew into his looks, as his features shifted tectonically with age, he was becoming ruggish, earthy, he'd even started growing a beard. Flora placed a cup of tea to his side, running her finger over the corner of his glasses, thinking, if she wanted to, she could crush them. The performance of love and the fire of it; an endless negotiation; a series of audience asides, of controlled explosions. As the evening drew in, Flora tied back her hair and put on a coat. 'It's silly you always driving,' he said stopping her, his suitcase bigger still. 'I'll just get a taxi.'

As he left, leaving behind the packed grapes, crime dramas on USB – treats she had prepared for his journey – Flora cried. At first, a tentative misting of the eyes, an overture, making way to gasping, flatulent sobs, big, glossy tears. The following weekend he didn't come home on the Friday evening and wasn't back until late Saturday afternoon. The weekend after that he didn't come home at all.

She started feeling closest to him sleeping; her waking thoughts and dreams meshing in an addled glue. She'd wake from a ferocious, thrashing sleep feeling like he was physically there, a garbling of non-sequiturs, a blizzard of scenes; conversations and events, impossible to pin down and immediately forgotten, but he was always there, every time she fell asleep, waiting for her. She preferred Dream Joseph to Real Joseph. Dream Joseph was reliable, preserved, packed in ice. Real Joseph was, well. 'I can't quite put my finger on it,'

Flora told her friend Casey, at Body Blow; a freshly acquired pastime, since the separation. Body Blow was a new fitness class at their gym; a human-shaped training bag, gender nonspecific, placed in front of each attendee, billed "Exorcise".

'Something's different.' She slugged her fist at a pillow-y circle, a resonating thwack punctuating her words. Joseph had been in London four months now. 'He seems distant on the phone, like he's not listening to anything I'm saying. Then suddenly he'll be really sweet. Last week he sent me an e-card. He called me his little donut hole.'

'Babe,' Casey replied, jogging on the spot, landing punches with a tiny grunt.

'It's another woman,' she wheezed. 'It's always another woman.'

They'd met several years ago at a party. Flora had taken ecstasy for the first time; a tight swell expanding in her stomach, a wriggling and writhing bliss, an artifice of joy fizzing around her head; yielding to a sudden weight, a sickly and terrifying weight. Staggering into an unfamiliar living room, peering at a waltzing brocade of light, she thought she might vomit. Beads of sweat slid from her forehead and she felt for something, for anything, to grab onto. She clutched an arm – Joseph's arm – and pulled him close. He held her at a distance, swept hair from her face and ran a finger beneath her eye. She watched him as if from afar, a blur beneath a twinkling haze; a blur that remained a blur, absent, abstract, always at arm's length. She remembered drinking a glass of water but didn't remember much else, though was later told he'd taken her home, sleeping on the floor beside her. The next morning he informed her someone had put something in her drink, and she should probably go to the police about it, or at least report it to the student support officer, maybe she should get checked out by her doctor. So creased was his consternation, so wide-eyed his belief that this thing, this little blonde thing,

31

with the pine framed *Roman Holiday* poster and the Carole King records bookended by oversized church candles, could not have voluntarily administered something so impure, so crass, as ecstasy; she hadn't the heart to correct him. 'You're right,' she replied, flattening her hair, rubbing make-up from her face. 'I'll report it to the university. And I'll book a doctor's appointment on Monday.'

How was she supposed to know this thin sliver of untruth, this morsel of fiction, was being dispensed to her future husband, the future love of her life, to grow fat, to develop wings. She hadn't realised she was signing such a lengthy contract with this small fabrication, but then, she hadn't yet realised lies take effort, they take commitment. She hadn't yet realised that if you're not in it for the long haul, well, best not to bother at all. She hadn't yet realised that in a relationship, honesty was just one of many options, a sort of moral high ground, yes, but no more so than vegetarianism or recycling. And she was both a vegetarian and a recycler. And so it took flight, Joseph showing her newspaper clippings with drink spiking statistics, sagely nodding towards public service posters. At their wedding, he'd toasted, 'Of course she only spoke to me because she was on Class A drugs! And before anyone says anything, it wasn't me who put it in her drink! But I'd like to raise my glass to whoever did!' On hearing his niece had been molested by a teacher on a school trip, he'd volunteered her counsel, telling his brother 'Flora had a near identical experience, I'm sure she'd be happy to help.'

'Near identical?!' she'd exclaimed as he slipped his phone back into his pocket. 'How exactly have I had a near identical experience?'

'Well,' he replied. 'Yours was a near miss.'

So regularly did this spiked drink motif recur, she often suspected he knew she'd taken the pill all along and they were both complicit in a lengthy sort of private joke. Her mind arched back to that bleary morning, his furrowed concern, his voice so deliberately tempered. She thought of him handing her a coffee, telling her the caffeine would annul any trace of hallucinogens in her system; how, when she rubbed her face and said she must look horrendous, he replied, 'You look beautiful.' How he had meant it. No, it couldn't be another woman. She was the liar, the deceiver, the fraud.

They booked a weekend away, to the countryside, to get a bit of fresh air; Joseph drove while Flora pressed her forehead against the glass, intimate with her dewy reflection. Paragliders hovered above the hills, floating nail clippings against the brilliant blue sky. How strange that England should have mountains, Flora thought. How gauche. They checked into a chintzy B&B, sprawling out on the velvet bedding. They went walking through the hills, faces damp and flushed, finishing with a butternut squash stew and mashed potatoes. They had lethargic, languorous sex. Watching him sleep, his back smooth and grey in the dark, Flora traced the names of former lovers onto his spine: Daniel, Simon, Guy From The Library, then, feeling particularly bold, spelt out their names and her fondest memory; Daniel, drunk in Liverpool; Simon, eating cereal, watching *The Wonder Years*; The Guy From The Library, abs. She wondered what her fondest memory of Joseph was and ran her hand through his hair. 'Sometimes,' she whispered. 'I just want to punch you in the face.'

'What?' he asked, opening his eyes. 'What did you just say?'

'Nothing,' Flora replied, turning over. 'I said nothing.' The next morning they were brought breakfast in the room, waking Flora, interrupting Joseph who was up, writing a message on his phone. 'I'll get it,' he said, wrapping himself in a robe, making for the door. Flora rolled across the bed, peering up to see him arranging a cafetière in the adjoining room, laying out the cutlery. She tapped his phone, lighting up the message he was sending to a woman's name she didn't recognise; an email about their trip. It was very wordy. It was very *written*. Recherché? she thought. Where the hell did he learn a word like recherché? He called her and she quickly set the phone aside. 'Well,' she said, sitting at the table, picking up a miniature chocolate croissant, turning it over in her fingers. 'Isn't this recherché?'

He came home at Christmas; they spent the holiday together in lieu of visiting family. Flora shuffled to the living room on Christmas morning, to find Joseph up and dressed, attached to his laptop once more. 'Don't do any work today,' she said, slipping onto his knee, winding her arms around his neck. 'It's Christmas.' He closed the lid. 'You're right,' he replied, wiggling out from beneath her. They prepared a homemade nut roast, toasting hazelnuts, crumbling stilton, grating parsnips in a silent communion. After they'd eaten the roast, Flora trotted to the kitchen, reaching for the back of the fridge. 'Linzer Torte!' she said. 'Do you remember how many we ate of these in Austria?!' Joseph rubbed his stomach, contriving large, swirling circles. 'I'm trying to watch my weight,' he replied as Flora removed a slice, covering it in a thick layer of whipped cream, eyeing him warily. He returned to his laptop, on the settee, defeated, she spooned a dollop of cake and cream into her mouth, a soggy cloud, feeling it squelch beneath her teeth.

They exchanged presents late in the afternoon, Flora gifting a boxy selection of paperbacks, a knitted blanket she'd been working on for the best part of a month. 'This is so you don't get cold on the train home,' she said, kneading it in her palm. 'This is so you don't forget me.' Joseph presented her with a small, flat square. Flora peeled back the papery wrapping, removing a long gold chain weighted down by a single charm, a tiny telescope, dangling delicately from her fingers. 'It's beautiful,' she said, swinging it back and forth, holding it up to her face, pretending to peer through it. 'Now I can keep an eye on you.' She clipped it around her throat. 'I'm going to wear it all the time.' Joseph ran his thumb across the bitty ornament. 'I knew you'd like it,' he yawned, kissing her forehead.

They slept off dinner, lying side by side, in their bedroom. Flora woke first, staring at Joseph, wondering about his thoughts, his dreams, wishing herself small, so small, she could crawl into his ear, to explore, to investigate. When Joseph's eyes opened, Flora squeezed hers shut, pretending. She lay still a while, waiting for him to get up, finally peeping to see if he'd fallen back asleep. On opening her eyes, she caught him blinking his shut, the same theatrics, rolling over, exhaling loudly. She got out of bed and poured herself a glass of water, settling on the settee, staring out of the window. She noticed his laptop perched on the desk beside her. She pressed her palm to it and felt its gentle heat, an enticing heat, like a bubble bath. She slid it onto her knee, prising open the lid, running a finger across the mousepad, bringing it to life. An incoming email, the woman he'd emailed before. She read it through, a narrative sashaying in front of her; swaggering, each word an apéritif, calmly digested. She read it again and then shut the lid, returning the laptop to his desk and walked through to the bedroom. She watched him lying there, breathing in and out. So, she thought. This is my nervous breakdown. Joseph let out an ungainly snore and jerked his foot from beneath the duvet, and on instinct she leaned over and tucked his foot back in, slipping under the covers beside him. She wrapped both arms around his stomach, nuzzling her face into his back, pressing her nose into his shoulder blade. He smelled of mint shower gel and mouthwash. Of Christmas dinner and coffee. Of the North and the South and everything in between. She held him close and shut her eyes, feeling that they were sinking into the bed, and then through the bed, and into the ground, sinking further and further down. She gripped him tighter, because what is it really, this thing, this small written thing, gone with the click of a button, the collapse of a screen, vanished, gone.

Beautiful Existence

It begins, and ends, with the birds.

A chirruping chorus, scattered squeaks trilling through the rustle; the branches carousing like veins, and on every branch a bird. 'My alarm clock,' I might say if I had someone to say it to. I'd pause at the word though. Alarm.

They are up before me, bobbing and twitching, pipping like flirts. They are a terrible roommate; with their squawking and their hollering, with no respect for emotional space, no respect for sleep. They are right gossips; cheeping secrets, who did what with who, and how. They are fat ballerinas. They are out-of-tune chanteurs. They are worse than that. They are – morning people. And like all morning people, they never let you forget it.

Mornings are hard. I suppose they're not hard for everyone; but they are hard for me. 'Task-based learning,' they told me. 'It's good to have a routine.' Mornings are all routine, all to-do; action-by-action, moment-through-moment; nudging you closer to the end of the day. The birds don't understand mornings; and I am as lumpen as old Quasimodo, all eyelid gristle and under-water movement, some late-Victorian curmudgeon, crying: 'The birds!', as I wave a weakly clenched fist at the window.

The birds!

Our appointment is at noon.

'A woman in Seattle,' I tell him, 'ate only Starbucks for a year.'

'Five hundred dollars a month and she never took a day off. She changed her name to Beautiful Existence.'

'You've got to admire the chutzpah.'

He taps his pen three times to his notepad. He is a man of logic, a man of reason, a Man Of Science; and what logical men don't understand is that logic is soothing to no one but them, pragmatism a useless arsenal, reason a crappy opiate.

'What does this have to do with the birds?' he asks.

'Well,' I reply. 'They are everywhere.'

He searches the room, furnished in olives and tangerines, litmus colours befitting of his trade.

'They are everywhere,' I repeat.

He taps at his notepad again.

'See you next week,' he says. 'I'm upping your prescription to twenty.'

I stop at reception; the receptionist is one of those coloured tights and cardigan girls. She makes marmalade and has bouncy hair. She wears mismatched socks and takes photographs of the leaves. She has a boyfriend. I mean, I presume she does.

'Same time?' she says. I look at her necklace: a tiny gold swallow nested in the dip of her throat.

Everywhere.

I slip three glossy magazines from the desk into my bag. 'Same time,' I say. When I'm outside, I trash them.

I go to the park.

I sit at the bench in the centre. Around me joggers weave figures of eight. A woman nibbles sunflower seeds. A mother chases twins in matching maroon mittens and black chequered hats; they are harnessed and reined, cables ejected from her wrists, like Spiderman. And then there are the birds; whistling in the trees, stitched on the sides of canvas bags; there are the birds.

Everywhere they are. Coffee shop sign. Put a bird on it. Light summer sweater. Put a bird on it.

It starts to rain, a single drop, slapping against my skin like an embarrassing sex sound; then it heaves, buckets of it, industrial containers of it, a whirring white sound, zeroes and ones, coded strings sloshing down. I walk home drenched.

At home I undress. I run a bath and listen to the news. I order takeout and cut off all my hair. I think about Beautiful Existence, with her slow roast pork and her poppyseed muffins and her gingerbread latte; and think: maybe I'll do that. Maybe that's the key.

The evenings are getting longer, stretching out like sleeping cats, rolling over and over. I count down to bedtime but it feels like it might never arrive.

It is dead quiet at night, a blank wash of silence, a still lake of no sound. The bed becomes giant in the dark, a puffed landscape, and me, a pointless Thumbelina, trying to make sense of the duvet. Time compresses. Time expands. Time stops being time. Everything feels bloated and make-believe.

But it ends. It does end. It ends with the birds.

They peep and bristle, hopping at their stations, chirruping their song. They jump and swoop, soaring into the air, gliding across the sky. They trill and leer, whooshing past my window, jettisoning into the blue, then falling weightlessly, falling, falling. This is how you do it, they sing. You just let go.

It's A Shame About Ray

Ray had given up answering questions. There seemed to be, he thought, too many of them. Best to just go with the flow. Be that guy; some easy-going dude, in sunglasses and a papaya print shirt. That guy didn't hit fifty, take up jogging and have an embolism. That guy didn't split a dick trying to find decent asparagus, ambling around puzzled; all salt and pepper hair at the Sunday farmer's market. That guy embraced his paunch, the inescapable inevitabilities of age, the unconquerable ravages of existence, replying 'whatever you say, doc!' when asked by his GP if he'd considered cutting down on salt, then went straight out for burgers. That guy was alright. That guy was, as you might say, a cool guy.

'Hey, baby,' his wife called from the nursery. They'd always called each other baby, babe, babes; it was their thing, but now they had a living, breathing baby, there was a hesitation in it, something else that needed shifting. She was perched halfway up a ladder, holding the handle, her hair pulled into some vegetal tangle. What was she doing up there? – pawing at the ceiling like a mad thing, feet over the ground, like her body was some unbreakable, undamageable object. He imagined her falling, the slap of her skin and the crack of her bones, and felt jets of adrenaline surge to his heart, a geyser of dread; then recalled his persona, his cool guy schtick. 'What do you think?' she asked, fixing some paper birds, some whimsical mobile, over the cot. He held his hands up – I surrender! – shrugging his shoulders, flexing his face. The rehearsed gestures of the recently laidback. She fussed with it some more. The nursery was half-done, in flux. Vinyl wall stickers, scattered stars and half-moons, on the right, on the left, Anita Ekberg, head thrown back, breasts thrust forward, rhapsodic, in the Trevi

Fountain. Oh! – it had been quite the guest room.

It would take the weekend to finish the job, the transition near complete, the house almost fully baby-proof. 'We'll soon be set,' he'd said, regretting the phrase, which jarred, summoning images of insects set in amber, jelly tough as varnish. Whatever remained in the mould, doomed to stay there, forever.

He navigated the peripheries of the room, his feet pressing tenderly against the carpet. Since the baby's arrival, the household had changed. Changed not in the plastic bottles that were everywhere. Changed not in the breast pump that lingered to the side of the bathroom sink like a perplexing adult aid. Changed not in the used nappy containing a single brown blob, which remained on the countertop for hours; the nappy's frilled edges the split shells of a clam, the blob an offered pearl. No. The changes were more abstract, more semiotic. He increasingly found himself bumbling around in socks and soft clothes, feeling like some senile old fool, some forgetful old pop pops, a lost guest in his own home.

'Things,' his wife said, descending the ladder, with infomercial grace. 'We need things.'

Things were her latest demand. An abstract bric-a-brac she willed at random. Like the space around them was significant. Like it needed filling. It was as if she had plopped this squirming animation onto the planet and couldn't figure out why he too could not create something from nothing. Baby, we need things. Baby, we need stuff. Baby. Baby.

'You can get all this from the supermarket,' she said. 'I'll write you a list.'

She left the room, leaving him with the baby. He looked past him with blissful incomprehension. Babies, with their smug ignorance, their swaggering oblivion. How gladly and giddily they were bewildered. He was propped in the corner, moored to his mobile, with that glazed expression Ray had trained himself not to think too much about. A squidgy, unknowable tumour. A flesh thing. With shining white eyes, roly-poly wrists and the gurgling pomp with which he filled his nappy.

He started to whimper, a soft woollen whimper, as his wife called him from downstairs. Ray froze, unable to decide who to tend to first, mother or baby, apples or oranges. She returned upstairs handing him the list, picking up the baby, who immediately settled. Babies, Ray had concluded, were mostly stupid. But this they did understand. The implicit responsibility of their mothers for them.

Ray scanned the list. It seemed straightforward. 'See you later, honey,' he whistled, leaving, and she kissed him on the rough shadow of his cheek. He was trying to introduce honey into their hypocoristic vernacular. Honey was neutral. Honey had no further implications beyond sweetness.

Ray recently found supermarkets stressful. He was used to stress. Of course, he was used to stress. But it was a different kind of stress at the supermarket. Different to the scattered flotsam of swaddling on their living room floor. Other to the lockstitch zigzag of the rush hour drive. The wolfish snapping of the customers, the hummed din of the registers, unique to the shop floor. Life, Ray had decided, was exchanging one type of chaos for another.

He paced the aisles looking at all the things. The crackling packeted things. The primary-coloured cardboard things. So many things. All reaching out, wanting to be chosen. He felt like the world was perennially bulleting questions at him. At every turn there was another question; semi or skimmed, paper or plastic, cash or card; another question that needed an answer. Like the whole world was made up of two lost halves of a whole, searching for each other, eternally.

Beneath the requests for wood glue and mason nails, his wife had written 'one cooked chicken', he noticed, with some relief. There wasn't nuance in cooked chicken. There weren't gradations. You just picked the thing; you just picked the one thing. His wife had taken to eating chicken since the birth when she'd been practically vegetarian up until then. Ray assumed it was something primitive, something lunar he didn't understand; to do with nesting and menstruation. He, the man, sent out to score meat.

He approached the rotisserie, the chickens circling in front of him, roasting to a red gold crisp. He stared at them, entranced; the methodic spin of the rods, the earthy odour, broken, when he noticed the butcher in the background, yanking apart the legs of a pink, plucked chicken, forcing his hand inside, pulling out the giblets. Ray felt suddenly sick. He squatted, with his hands placed over his knees, the world a swirling Lazy Susan, swaying in tandem around him. He tried to forget the scene, as he had tried to forget the scene it reminded him of; his wife lying supine, her legs pulled apart, the baby dragged out of her. How they had treated her like a thing, a meat thing, to be cut up and hollowed out. It had been an awful birth. A day he would forever remember as the worst of his life. He retrieved his phone from his pocket, prodding its glassy surface, dialling home, thinking if he could just hear his wife's voice, if she could just give him some instructions, some direction, he'd be fine. 'Baby?' she said, over the thin crackle of static, the shitty supermarket reception. He had the feeling of trying to supress a cough, that convulsing heaving panic.

'Baby?'

On the way home Ray called in for a drink. It seemed like a cool guy move; a leisurely interval before they were set; elbows resting on the gravy polish of the pine bar, a single malt whisky cooling with two cubes of ice.

He sipped his drink, feeling the heat settle in his stomach, wondering why all comforts were thermal. The muted television flickered foreign atrocities, genocides Ray no longer felt pathos for. It was like grieving the seasons, pining the moon;

it was so far away, so abstract, it seemed senseless to engage. Even the television didn't look like a real-life television, like a television within a television, a film within a film, a dream within a dream, the way a life could feel like a life within some other life, some scripted, unknowable life, some non-linear narrative. Well flip the script, buddy! Ray thought. Spoil the ballot! Throw your homework onto the fire! – as he knocked back the last of his drink and considered asking the guy next to him whether we all saw the same colours. He ordered another drink, turning over the cocktail menu, thinking next he'd have a piña colada, easy on the piña, with a side of shrimp and fries.

He rubbed his face. The suggestion of stubble. The threat of it. Resonating a satisfying scratch. Like the ice chiming against his glass, the clack of high heels on a hardwood floor. A bar sound. One of his favourite sounds. He wandered to the jukebox, put on some music; Johnny Cash, Roy Orbison, Pete Seeger. Some cool guys. Some guys who got it. He returned to his seat and wiggled his glass at the waiter, the way he'd seen in movies, gesturing for another, and then another; stamping his feet in time to the songs. Dance like nobody gives a crap. Drink like you don't have a family to go home to. Love because what else is the point. By the time last orders arrived, he was a slop; as sloppy as an old sloppy joe, slopping everywhere, slopping his keys onto the carpet, slopping spittle from his jaw. What Ray learned about drink driving that night is that no one intervenes, no one steps in; like wildlife documentarians, they let nature take its course. And when he came to, his head pressed against the steering wheel, a pool of blood in his lap, flashes of blue from the corner of his eye, he thought, sometimes all you can wish for in life is the physical manifestation of pain.

He woke up in a hospital bed, handcuffed to the rail. It seemed unnecessary. He really wasn't going anywhere. He lifted up his free arm, bandaged, like lazy fancy dress. His hand had gone, removed; only a white stub remained. A giant q-tip. He told the nurse when he came to he didn't care; and he still didn't. What was a hand, anyway? Just another thing. Just another with or without. Everything was just a thing; there was no agency, no ability to affect change. It was the curse of the modern age, options; who needed options, when everything was essentially meaningless?

He thought of his wife during the birth. How he had watched her, her chest heaving up and down, like something equestrian, like something breathing because they meant it. Wondering how so much blood could come from one tiny human person. How he held the baby, but felt like he could be holding anything, any old thing, any old rock or piece of string.

He looked up; his wife hovered over him. It was the first time he had seen her since the accident.

'Baby?' she said. 'Are you alright, baby?'

She seemed like she wasn't really there; superimposed onto the scene, like the Cottingley fairies. She had this ghostly halo of gentleness about her; it was the thing he loved most, like she was from some other planet, lingering inter-dimensionally.

'Listen,' he replied. 'Can you stop fucking calling me baby?'

He couldn't bear to hear the word again.

He couldn't bear to say the word again.

Mother or Baby, they had asked. A simple question requiring a simple answer. Choose your own adventure. Complete your character arc. They stood facing him, mint green and masked, eyebrows expressing emergency. Like bit parts waiting for their line, waiting for their SAG card. Mother or Baby. Mother or Baby. And he had said Baby. It was instinctive. He didn't even recognise the voice that said it as his own. Decision made. He had let her go. Let her go like she was a thing. Bon voyage, sweetheart! See you on the other side.

Hospitals, he used to joke, were where you came when your body sprang a leak.

He'd registered some hurt, but it seemed insignificant, infinitesimal; a pinprick of pain amongst a swarming miasma of emotion.

One thing or the other; how could you choose between one thing or the other.

'Are you okay?' she repeated.

He looked past her, wanting to answer, wanting only to say the right thing.

He stared into the half-light beyond the hospital curtain, the corners gently heaving, in the clear corridor air. The lazily bleeping heart monitors, the silent hurry, the breathless calm, experienced as stop motion, snippets staggered, partially digested. His wife flickering in and out of focus. And a thought, somewhere, papered beneath the cracks, slippery and evasive and impossible to pin down; that everywhere, maybe, is exactly the same.

Dates

Dust shadow over your eyelids, a shade with some gorgeous, caloric name; blink as it loosens to cinders. Arrange curls that coil to your shoulders like the swooping slip of a helter skelter slide. Select underwear with the considered curation of triumph. Realise you have no good, clean underwear. Dating is an art, and like everything else, it is a bit hit and miss.

Prepare conversation topics, little flash cards fixed in your mind; things like responsive design and capitalist realism, in a pinch, bring up Syria; these are the things that will make you seem interesting, this here is your back-up plan.

Consider how you might pitch yourself; maybe like, a girly-girl, but one who can, you know, fix a car. Or perhaps something more throaty, more guttural, something perhaps, more Germanic; a country frau who might throw on a dirndl and enthusiastically milk a cow.

File your nails. Tidy your room. Wonder why you ever gave up smoking. Wonder why your steady shift dress, which previously fit like memory foam, is suddenly too small.

Arrive a little early, surveying the restaurant; the tables and chairs arranged in a peculiar gridlock, like a series of contained gameshows. Decide whether you are the contestant or the host. Be polite and ask questions. Ask a lot of questions.

When your food arrives, stare at your plate. It is a riddle that needs to be solv. It is a crossword that needs to be half-finished. It is a book that needs to be abandoned mid-way, its pages ruffling in the whistle of a light summer breeze.

Eat with a careful mathematics. Four bites of the caramelised cabbage. Two of the Cumbrian roast veal. Seven of the sorrel and split pea mousse. Like chromosomes in a human person; the numbers need to be exact.

Lara Williams

The waiter will loom over you. 'Is everything okay?' he will ask. Now there is a question. Now that there is a question.

Say something whimsical, something like; doesn't the light bounce off the walls like something that might have been seized by the Third Reich, something like, don't the rose jellies look like two bloodied kidneys, which do themselves, in turn, look like quotation marks; something like, doesn't the sound of you smacking your lips together when you chew make you want to stab out your own eyes with a salad fork.

Stare off into some wistful middle distance when you are saying it to instil the sentiment with the correct air of authenticity. Men like that.

Ignore the prickling pain when he says he doesn't like skinny girls. This is flattery. You are being flattered.

Split the bill. It is the twenty-first century. Now, come on.

Punctuate the evening with an insouciant punch on the arm, and some pally name, like buddy or cowboy; tell him you'll just get a cab.

Return home. Flip open your laptop. Microwave something to eat. Take up space. Consider why you are even trying to meet someone if you are happiest when left alone.

Treats

It was nearly fifteen years ago Elaine had stood peering toward the harlequin bustle of the fourteenth floor, doped by the static September heat, watching the glass panelling refract and scythe. It was one of those sneaky summer days, one that lounges around a chilled August, making a wild and unpredictable cameo, hoodwinking you into knits, swindling you out of sandals. She'd already taken to whispering 'you get to a certain age', to no one in particular; the tiny bones in her hand creaking like viola, shopping bags cutting into the skin of her wrists; whispering it beneath her breath, the words a smooth tonic.

You get to a certain age.

She was thirty-five.

Joan met her at reception, dressed head-to-toe in black, like some sort of devastating widow; her lips a woozy red, her foundation a flawless white facade. They took the lift, staring silently ahead, slim parallel lines, a vertical Hays Code, counting off the floors.

'Hot, isn't it?' Elaine ventured.

'Not especially,' Joan replied, buttoning her cardigan with a pointed elegance.

The office was a mess; a scatter of half-opened boxes, the cavalier architecture of a child's fort; the ceiling fan flickering off and on, the paint drying in patches. But Elaine saw its potential, the order in the olio, feeling the compact thrill of a nice meal or good art. Her thoughts had slowed to a plod in the heat, circling slowly, like the fish in the bowl her husband had gifted her. She grappled for half-formed ideas; wispy responses dispatched into the air, floating away like dandelions huffed into the wind. To her surprise, Joan offered her the job – Personal Assistant – and she rose to her feet, not quite knowing how to accept the offer, announcing 'Shall I just get us a cup of coffee?'; a conspicuous affirmation.

She was Officer Manager now, but still retained a few PA duties, picking up dry-cleaning here and there, swirling stevia into coffee. Everyone needed a bit of looking after. Even Joan.

Elaine liked to look out for people. She was a tall woman, and as a tall woman, she suspected she was made for it; made to protect, to watch over. Everything about her seemed to accommodate her height; her airy, echoing vowels, the swooning lumber with which she moved. But then she hit fifty, felt the uteral twangs, the telling hot flushes and fluctuations of mood, and realised her body wasn't made for height, for elevation; it was made, and had always been made, for menopause. She gained a little weight; developing a pleasing paunch she'd rub admiringly. She'd sit at the kitchen table breaking off squares of cooking chocolate. She rang her sister to say she wouldn't be coming home for Christmas, and while she was at it, could she stop being such a goddamn tramp her whole life. She had crème-de-menthe with dinner. She listened to Cher. She booked a trip to the Peak District alone.

Her husband wondered what the hell had gotten into her. He'd curse and rumble, rolling his eyes at her elasticated waistbands, ask her why she'd stopped wearing make-up. But it didn't bother her; things were looking up for old Elaine!

'You want to take an old girl to the cinema?' she asked.

'Not especially,' he replied. 'But I will.'

'Old woman,' he said, after a pause. 'Old *woman.*'

Elaine got in early to leave a plastic pot of maraschino cherries, and a small bottle of vodka, on Joan's desk. Performing secret good deeds was a guilty pleasure for Elaine; a covert joy, a sort of private joke, really, shared only with herself. She would perform secret good deeds, flush with joy, made glad by the baffled delight they'd bring. She'd slip ten pound notes into charity buckets. She'd pay for drinks. She'd order slices of cake, have them presented to young couples, watching them across the café. She occasionally imagined secret good deeds were being performed for her; imagining the world fluent in a silent language of kindness. Upon finding an apple on her car bonnet, a Pink Lady, as yellow and red as the sun, beaming a smiling curve of white light, she thought: Who left this for me? What lovely person left me this? before noticing the rest of the car, a punnet of raspberries smeared across the windscreen, an orange squelched into the numberplate, and a note, tucked and fluttering, beneath the wipers.

Can you keep your fucking car out of the loading bay?

But the slow drag of disappointment had grown numb, hard, like a frozen waterfall, it barely registered. There were things to get excited about in this life. Things to thrill for. Like zumba and sugared almonds. Water aerobics and flavoured liqueur. Cher.

At three she popped out to get Joan some lunch. She selected a smoked salmon bagel and an iced tea. At the till, John The Sandwich guy, literally the name of his business, slipped a French tart into her bag. Elaine smiled. A big screwball smile. As big and sinking as the Titanic.

'Thanks, John,' she said. 'You're a good egg.'

'*You're* a good egg!' he replied, chuckling floridly. 'An Ananov egg! A Fabergé egg! Eggs Benedict!'

She left giggling, letting the door click softly behind her, and the thought suddenly struck her, as occasionally it did; that she didn't have a single true friend in all the world.

She got home to the smell of pizza, the sound of the seaside tinkering from the television. She located the pizza box, a paper white square, balanced on top of the kitchen table; promising slicks of grease and steam marbling the lid. She teased it open, knowing already there would be none left, and made instead for the fridge compiling a plate of leftovers. She ate at the kitchen table, watching the fish circle its bowl, the seventh fish, she thought, Moby Dick the seventh. She set down her fork to sprinkle fish food onto the water, pink and orange flakes, that had the texture and smell of chicken stock. She felt subversive, transgressive; radicalising the food chain like that. The fish wriggled hurriedly to the waterline, its orange mouth nipping sweetly at the surface, its big black eyes, frozen in a kind of permanent disbelief, a doubtful and necessary trust.

Once, she had wanted kids. And then she wanted a kid. Then she wanted a cat. But now she was fully committed to this; a solitary goldfish, eternally circling the left hand corner of their kitchen table. She looked at the goldfish, swimming and flickering, the little hinges of its jaw, chomping up and down. She loved it, she thought, in the smallest, saddest way. She wanted to fish it out, to feel it in her palm, to stroke its slick, twitching body and feel its satin soft fins.

She finished her food, depositing her plate into the sink and made her husband a cup of tea. She placed it on the carpet next to his feet, on the flattened pale ring of shag, kissing his head as she went to bed.

'Wait,' he called. 'What do you want for your birthday?'

She paused between the top and the bottom, stasis on the stairs, fingering the covered buttons of her jersey.

'Just your health and happiness,' she replied. She thought he'd forgot.

'And a million dollars.'

'How about that trip to the cinema?' he said.

'Well that would be nice,' she replied, thinking she wouldn't be able to sleep with all this excitement flip-flopping in her heart.

She worked on her birthday. She always worked on her birthday. There were things to be done! – papers to file, phone calls to make. Plus Joan needed looking after; at eleven she would deliver her morning cappuccino, at one she'd remove the cherry tomatoes from her salad, at four she'd make her lemon and ginger tea, past six, she needed to be told to go home. There was a catharsis in it. There was a ceremony. It was a full-time job. It was literally a full-time job! Elaine made time to treat herself too; treats could save a person, she thought. 'Treat yourself every day,' her mother had told her, and she did; taking herself on little walks, an expensive haircut here and there. Once, her husband had treated her, courted her; whisked her off to restaurants, showed her off to his friends. Now her treats were reserved for her birthday; and even then, they didn't always manifest.

At the end of the day, Joan called her in, asking if she'd shut the door behind her. 'Don't think I forgot,' she said, beckoning Elaine over. She thought Joan looked more pale, more delicate in the milky evening light. She wondered if she was getting enough iron. Joan gestured at a brown parcel, tied with string, propped amongst the scattered jetsam of admin on her desk. 'That's for you,' she said, and Elaine began unwrapping the parcel, pulling back the folds. 'What are you doing?' Joan said. 'That needs couriering. Tonight.' Elaine blushed, a hot pink hue, arching her nose and cheekbones. She resealed the package and tucked it beneath her arm. She could drop it off on the way to the pictures.

She removed her coat from the back of her chair, swinging her bag across her shoulder, noticing her phone flashing, a staccato red reminder. Voicemail. Her husband. Delivering a flimsy excuse for cancelling their plans. She returned the phone to its cradle, sat back in her chair and thought about her life. It was like the time she went to an art gallery, expecting something grandiose, something moving, something, perhaps, profound; swampy colours, powdery paintings of girls in profile. Instead she found hokey sculptures, marble penises extending from the corners. 'Where's the art?' she'd said. 'Is that the art?' Being given salt when you wanted sugar.

An olive not a grape. That was it, she thought. That was her life all over.

She waited in line at the cinema, she'd decided to go alone; though her irritation lingered, like a stubborn base note of leather or sage. She looked at the people queuing around her; couples, mostly, but a few people on their own, also. At the front desk she asked for a ticket for herself and another for the young girl behind her, a fellow solo cinema goer, nervously thumbing the lapel of her coat. She asked that they just give her the ticket; no fuss made, no details given. She left the desk, her own ticket printed and folded in the palm of her hand. She thought about the young girl, thought about how surprised she might be, about how nice it was to be treated.

She thought about all the nice things people had done for her, from historic dates with her husband to the brief moment she saw that apple, perched on her car; how her heart had skipped a beat like it might leap out of her chest. She thought she'd treat herself to some popcorn, and a hotdog too, taking up the space around her, stretching out her arms and legs, and enjoying the film. She thought about how it was her birthday, and not a bad one at that, and her heart did a little leap on its own; you could do that, to your own heart, you could be so kind to yourself you could make your own heart leap.

After all, she thought; what goes around comes around.

Taxidermy

At twenty-eight Neala lost her boyfriend. At twenty-nine she lost her job. At thirty she lost her full head of hair.

Her boyfriend left one Sunday afternoon, an otherwise ordinary Sunday; and so the breakup felt like something rather perfunctory, some chore he felt obliged to complete, like taking out the bins or finishing the washing up. 'I'm leaving you,' he said, as they sat on separate sofas, reading the papers, coffee cooling in their laps. Neala tore a page from the food and drink supplement, wafting it in his general direction; a coterie of croissants and cake, of biscuits and brioche; the hoodwinking and hairspray; the nulling, gratifying trickery of broadsheet food photography. 'Chocolate nut cookies,' she said. 'This is what I'm going to bake today.' She put on a coat and went to the shops to buy ingredients; eggs and butter, white chocolate and macadamias, saying nothing else. When she got back he'd started packing, the flat partially autopsied, cardboard boxes and gym bags littering the floor. She ignored them, busying herself in the kitchen, melting butter to a sunshine sizzle, swirling eddies of melted chocolate into the mix. She put them in the oven, set the timer for fifteen minutes, then went to the bathroom to be sick. By the time the cookies were ready, he was leaving. 'Aren't you going to have a cookie?' she said. 'Well I suppose I'll have one,' he replied, taking one, taking the biggest one, eating it, eating the whole thing standing there in front of her, staring at the gradually pooling tears in the corners of her eyes. 'Don't cry,' he said. 'One day you will see that this was for the best.'

The job followed. She started turning up late, tired, and one time, drunk. Still drunk from the night before, wearing an outfit that could only be the sartorial judgement of the still inebriated. 'We need to talk,' her boss said. 'About your performance.'

'I'm sorry,' Neala replied. 'But I think you've mistaken me for someone who gives a fuck.'

And then it was the hair; when the hair started falling out, it seemed almost inevitable, the big reveal, the punchline, the showstopper. Was she even surprised? More perplexed as to why it hadn't happened sooner. After one thing ejected itself from you, the rest, she found, followed.

The hair was, in many ways, the greater loss; at least on a day-to-day level. It was her only indulgence; a single source of vanity; buoyant loops twirling giddily around her shoulders, glossy tendrils hanging like fat noodles. For a time, she wore a wig, but couldn't stand removing it, removing her hair, along with her make-up at night, to slip under the sheets like a big, bald baby. And so she would wrap her head in a silk scarf, sometimes tying it in a knot above her forehead, like a turban, other times fastening it at the nape of her neck, like a low ponytail. Sometimes she would catch a glimpse of herself and think she looked almost elegant, but the thought was fleeting, like a fleck of dust that hangs in the air, impossible to catch.

On her mother's advice, she took up a hobby; taxidermy, enrolling on a course at her local college. Making dead things look nice, there was a poignancy in that, there was a catharsis. She learned to prepare, to stuff, to treat and mount small birds and rodents, wiring their wings into celestial spans, positioning their feet into stances. Her friends would collect roadkill, wrapping them in plastic bags, passing them to her furtively, in artisanal coffee shops. Her freezer was full of them; mice, finches, on a few occasions, hamsters, gifted from her friend Stacie, a primary school teacher tasked with keeping alive the school pet. She loved her new hobby, it made her feel artistic and wild; unburdened with work, she felt like a true bohemian, with her bald head and coarse, chemical calloused fingers. She felt like she had shed layers of herself and gotten to her core.

She felt great.

On her tutor's suggestion, she started teaching taxidermy, facilitating workshops at a school for marginalised teenagers; their eyes luminescent. 'Look!' they would call over to her, giddily displaying their wares; voles in sunglasses, house sparrows in top hats.

She decided to move, wanting somewhere cheaper, somewhere more humble, more manageable, and started renting a room from an elderly couple, on the outskirts of town. It was a small room but it was comfortable; she'd leave the window open at night, feeling the crisp breeze on her naked scalp, the broth-y scent of Terry and Margaret's cooked chicken carrying from the kitchen. She stopped wearing headscarves. This is me, she thought. And I have nothing to hide.

Her ex-boyfriend called. He wanted to check up on her, to make sure she was doing okay. He felt bad, he said, about how things had ended. 'Oh, but I am great,' she said. 'You were right. About it being for the best.' But the exchange left her cold, wheedling into her heart and head, and she started thinking it might actually be nice. It might be nice to have somebody again. To have somebody to care about. To have somebody to call. 'Would you ever get back together with him?' Stacie asked. 'Would I?' she replied, considering it, turning it over, flipping it upside down like a pancake with a hideous underside.

Leaving her class one evening she balanced an owl she had been tinkering with on her car bonnet; the wings wired into a dazzling display, her canvas bag jostling utensils at her side. She recognised one of the teachers she had spoken to occasionally in the staff room. She thought he was very nice. A snappy dresser with a great sense of humour. 'What's this?' he asked, raising an eyebrow, hovering at the car parked next to her. She felt herself blushing, telling him she taught taxidermy, this was her current project, that she'd brought it in to show her students. 'That's cool,' he said. She'd never been called cool before. She'd never been called cool even once before. 'Maybe I'll see you around,' he finished, and she giggled and got in her car. 'Maybe,' she replied. 'Maybe.'

She backed up and drove off, watching him reflected in her wing mirror, he was tall and dark, dapper in a maroon chequered shirt, and pointed, brown leather brogues.

He leant against his car and lit a cigarette; watching her in silhouette, disappear down the road. He thought about what pretty eyes she had. What a lovely voice she had. How cool it was that she taught taxidermy. Thinking what a shame, such a damn shame, it was, that she had no hair.

Penguins

She finds herself single, twenty-nine, partially-employed and about a half a stone overweight. Roller dexter of eligible friends rattling thin. Thirties breathing down her neck like an inappropriate uncle. She jogs. Looks good in turquoise. Finds herself punctuating gas 'better out than in!' patting her stomach like a department store Santa.

She mopes, watches television, develops a taste for medjool dates, shoving handfuls into her mouth, sticking to her gums like toffee. This is who I am, she thinks. Mouth full of brown. Cackling into the night.

She starts making people uncomfortable. The sarcasm, the cynicism, the general aura of malaise, heck even the gas, were alright on somebody engaged, cute even, but on a single woman who it must be said is not getting any younger. Well.

'You'll meet someone,' her friends tell her. 'The right guy's out there I just don't know where!' They say this exasperated. Some old fuddy duddy searching for their glasses.

She notices less invitations. Her iCal yawns blank. She wonders what she ever did before. How the hell did she spend her time? She runs into people. Into her old gangs. 'Oh, you're all here!' she says, hurrying out like a diseased thing, her gaze darting around the spaces at the sides of the walls.

She resolves to do dating websites. Dating websites are something she does now. She doesn't like them. The romantic ones anyhow. The ones with cupid or soulmates in the URL. Those are not the ones for her. But the fish one she likes. She enjoys its wilful cynicism. All just fish we are. Sling enough shit at the wall and something's got to stick.

A few days in she starts to get messages. Men message her. All kinds of men! Though mainly tights fetishists, role-players and one time a Tory. It is hard to imagine which is worse. 'How are you?' they begin. They can't help but notice she likes Murakami. Has she heard of *This American Life*? They bet she'd get a real kick out of that. And what about tights? Does she wear tights? What about fishnet tights? What about two pairs of tights? Has she got any photographs of herself wearing tights or could she perhaps take some? She did not realise there were so many sub-genres to tights fetishism. If nothing else she has gained this.

'Hey,' says some guy, fringe flopping in front of his eyes. He seems promising. Better looking than the others. Hey yourself she thinks, tilting back her head, angling forward her laptop, concluding what she likes about him is how he stands. She looks at his photos like they are a really nice meal.

They meet ostensibly for coffee knowing they'll have sex if the opportunity arises. But they do have coffee. Icelandic coffee! They also have cake. The cake makes her feel sick but then a lot of things do.

'You wouldn't believe the weirdos I have messaging me,' she tells him, cutting through the sponge and buttercream with the side of her fork. He is flattered. He is flattered not to be one of the weirdos. She gets drunk and laughs a lot. She laughs the sort of laugh that gets away from you. One that needs to be lassoed back.

They go back to hers. She has an HDMI cable and Netflix and two thirds of a bottle of wine. She fixes him a drink. They sit on opposite ends of the sofa. Neither turns on the television. They inch closer and he rests his head on her shoulder. It is a bit awkward but aside from anything it is logistically awkward and uncomfortable. She lifts his head and turns it round like the prop skull from *Hamlet*, kissing him with a straightforward matter-of-factness while he pushes his hand up her skirt. After, he fetches tissue paper from the bathroom, wiping her stomach like he is nursing a wound.

He meets her friends. He is polite. He places a hand on

her shoulder when they make fun of her for having never seen *Chinatown*. He buys them a round of drinks. He talks to Kate about the guy she is seeing. 'That guy's a jerk,' she hears him say. She smiles. Lying in bed she thinks: he likes me. She rests her head on his chest, listening to his heart contract and expand, pumping out what was left, making room for her. In the morning they have sex. He looks like he wants to say something. 'What?' she asks.

'Nothing,' he says. Red faced. Breathless.

'What?' she asks again. 'Am I doing something wrong? Would you like me to do something else?'

He kisses her forehead, untangles her hair. 'Everything you're doing is fine.'

They go to an art gallery. She wears a backpack and jeans. She looks at him. He is wearing a backpack and jeans. She looks at the other couples in the art gallery. They are all wearing backpacks and jeans.

'Come on,' she says. 'Let's get a drink.'

One night he prods her shoulder. 'I love you,' he says, like he is polishing off a truth. Just saying what he sees. Handing her a heart shaped box and now she has to figure out its compartments, learn how to flip the lid. A house she has to furnish, to keep clean. 'I love you too,' she says, regretting adding too. A cop out. A disgrace.

'Would you like to meet my parents?' he asks. 'And we should go away.' There is a long inventory of things to do. They dine with other couples, touring their friends. They take turns to make food. A lot of being in a relationship, she realises, is negotiating what you are going to have for tea.

'I have something to ask you,' he tells her, one night, sat on the settee. They eat curry with coconut rice. Couple of posh yoghurts waiting for afters. She nods and chews.

'It's about. Um. Sex.' She begins to worry. She is not as limber as she once was. What she likes now is when it's over soon.

'Ok,' he says. 'Here goes.'

'I would like you to dress up like a penguin and incubate some eggs.'

She recalls something she read about improv. Yes. And. That was the ethos. She realises how heavily this has informed her worldview.

'Yes,' she says. 'And lets us eat this yogurt.'

She researches. Obviously, she researches. 'You know it is typically the male penguin who incubates the egg though they often take turns,' she tells him at the self-checkout in Asda.

'Jesus,' he says. 'Can this not wait until we're outside?'

'Ok,' she replies, adding quietly under her breath, 'Do you want me to be the male penguin or the female one?' He pretends not to hear. She wonders if it is just the one egg that needs incubating or multiple eggs. She watches him walk out the shop door.

'I love you!' she yells, the automatic doors snapping shut. She has a lot of questions.

At his flat they wash the dishes and he tells her it is more of an abstract fantasy. The detail is not of importance. She disagrees. In this situation perhaps more so than in any other situation she has ever encountered in her life the detail seems to be of absolute importance.

'Let's just drop it,' he says. 'Let's pretend I never brought it up.' He is wearing marigolds. They are not attractive.

At work she obsessively Googles penguins. She tries to find them erotic. They are handsome, she supposes, though handsome like a smart drinks cabinet as opposed to a really strong jaw. She wonders if the whole world has lost its mind.

She pulls on her pyjamas while he scrolls through his phone. 'What if I paint my face?' she suggests. 'What if I paint my face black? Or would that be too racial?' This sort of thing, she believes, is about compromise. He exhales loudly leaving the room. He does not say no.

Walking through town she watches a teenager spit at a

middle-aged man outside Argos.

'Did you see that?' she asks, fingernails digging into his arms, face urgently over his shoulder.

'People are absolutely awful to each other. To a person they are horrible twats.'

'You,' he says, rolling his eyes. 'You can be so cynical.'

'It's not being cynical,' she replies, 'if you're constantly being proven right.'

In the evenings they watch documentaries. Music documentaries. Serial killer documentaries. Documentaries about the state of the automobile industry in Detroit. They make Thai food. They make Mexican. They take it in turns to stir the soup. Gradually, they stop mentioning the penguins.

The lease runs out on his flat and so they move in. It makes sense. Her flat is much bigger than his and it's cheaper that way. He has a lot more stuff than she does. She throws out all her CDs and most of her books. Makes room in her drawers. Empties her cupboards. When she looks through her wardrobe for something to wear his pressed and dry-cleaned tuxedo stares at her like a joke.

She starts going to bed earlier than him. She needs more sleep than he does. At night, in bed, she takes to wondering things. Why it is the male penguin that incubates the eggs. Why a teenager would spit at a man. Why he even owns a tuxedo. Why every time she says I love you it is with an upwards inflection.

Toxic Shock Syndrome

Jennifer had been to a hospital only once before. Age fourteen. Her first use of a tampon. Toxic Shock Syndrome.

She committed to using a tampon from her first ever period. It was at that same time she got big. Puberty kicked in and her metabolism conked out; and she grew and grew, spilling into the space around her. Since then people were always telling her she was big; big heart, big smile, big personality, big the lot. Just generally, abstractly big. There was no reference to her body though it was implicit. Skated around like a pivot. Something that needed acknowledging or pointing at, though indirectly so. Her period congenitally, inexorably linked. That big heart of hers pumping blood around and out of her body; leaking it like an excess, like stuff to spare. There was something more uncomfortable about big women menstruating. Something presumed to ooze. It felt shameful and as she stared at the rich red blood pooling in her sanitary napkin she acquiesced to stop the slop at the source; forcing a super plus tampon into her (likely) large vagina.

She hadn't always been big. As a child she was delicate, nimble, quick on her feet. She had an ethereal quality. She could get into small spaces. For a long time she still felt like that same slip of a thing; running her hands over where her hipbones used to be, sitting with the elegance of the impossibly tiny. But gradually she came to accept her new size; the knowledge sitting inside her like a foreign object. Unwelcome, though very much there.

But she did not feel sprawling or vast, she felt composed; as perfectly contained as palms pressed together. She gave nothing away. There were no leakages, no ooze. You saw of her only what she wanted and she was judicious about that.

And yet lying in bed feeling the weight of herself push down into the mattress there was no denying it; she'd occupied more mass than that to which she was entitled and she'd never even been given a choice.

'Jenny,' her doctor told her. 'Jenn.' People were always sawing off bits of her name, reducing it, making it neat and pretty where she liked its entirety. Its needless sprawl. Its somewhat awkward prosody. Jennifer, she would correct them. JENNIFER. She'd wanted some valium for a flight. Not because of nerves or fear, just something to knock herself out, to get it over with. 'Is this because of your size?' her GP enquired. 'Wear flight socks. You can get them in Asda.'

Her size recurred again and again as cause over effect. The supposed route of all her pain. When she fell over at work, slapping her spine against the dense marble of the office reception, peeling back her jumper to reveal the flesh, pink and bruised, her resultant back problems were denoted by the GP as 'more to do with your size'. When she began feeling light headed, lacking in energy, before her blood tests revealed an acute B12 deficiency, she was told she 'probably just needed to lose some weight'.

People, she realised, liked women small. Something to be dangled from their wrist. Slipped neatly inside their pocket. And as she boarded the plane, noticing with some reservation she'd been given the middle seat, she sat down, feeling her thighs squeeze beneath the armrests at her side, her bottom packed in and oppressed. Though flipping through the in-flight magazine she thought about the cool egalitarianism of the sky. Up in the air everyone was weightless as a cloud. A man in a smart suit stopped and took the window seat beside her. She stood up to tell him to pass, subjected to the ludicrous rigmarole again. He was a businessman, she supposed, a salient salt and pepper type, all blow-dried hair and Michael Douglas gesticulations. He caught her looking over at him. He looked pleased.

She was glad he was sat next to her. He made her feel safe. There was something loaded about the person you were sat next to on a flight. Tipping on the precipice of reason and stupidity, the profound and the perfunctory. Floating in a big metal juggernaut on only thin air. The numbers just don't add up! If you were going down, you were going down together. Looking around the fuselage, she hated the pomp and gesture that accompanied flying. The romcoms and crackers, the wet wipes and cheap perfume; all of it, all a distraction, smoke and mirrors eclipsing the fact – just watch to whom you say smoke. After take-off she ordered a large gin and tonic, sinking her Valium, the only sensible course of action, her body soupy and relaxed, dozing in her seat.

She woke a few hours later, to the white noise of the engine, the syncopated giggle of the passengers, plugged in and tuned out. She noticed the hand of the man next to her, pressed idly against her knee. She looked over seeing he was fast asleep. She wondered whether she should move his hand, or her legs, place them to one side, though found his touch comfortable, a little thrilling, really. She pulled out her novel from the seatback and began reading, sensing the slightest movement – the back of his palm splayed out and moving with the faintest pressure against her. She looked at him again. He seemed still to be sleeping. She continued reading, her leg remained in situ. Then she felt a slow, deliberate graze, his fingers moving pleasurably against her skin, moving up and down, circling round and round. If he began to slow, she nudged him a faint twitch of encouragement. He continued moving his hand again, his fingers creeping beneath her thighs, so she was essentially sitting on his hand. He pushed further beneath her. Her underwear was damp. She looked around, at the flight attendants, the passengers, enjoying her own audacity. She didn't care. She felt wonderful, some gorgeous creature to be pleasured, his arm moving rhythmically beneath her. She bit her lip feeling sensual and desired, rocking gently in her seat, matching his rhythm. She was close. She was halfway there when he suddenly stopped. She looked over at him, he was gasping for air, his chin thrust forward, his face reddening by the moment. She called for help.

'He can't breathe!' she yelled. 'He can't breathe!'

A stewardess hurried over, forcing Jennifer out of her seat. She stood up leaving his hand limp and white in the seat beneath her. 'Were you sitting on his hand?' the stewardess cried.

'Why were you sitting on his hand?!'

There was a ruckus. Things move quickly when a person might die. There were no whiskey sours or ham paninis, now; just the gooey throb of your own heartbeat, the beast roaring beneath the soles of your feet. Jennifer studied the little graphic of the plane pulsing across the screen. They made an emergency landing in Madrid. A flight attendant asked if she knew him, if she'd like to travel with him to the hospital. The notion was a lunatic one, but also, a strange necessity. She trailed some time after the ambulance in a taxi. All that desire left looping in the sky.

At the hospital she bought a *National Geographic* and a packet of Doritos. She thought about the one other time she'd sat in a hospital waiting room, her temperature soaring over a hundred before they'd check her in. How she'd felt light as a feather doped up on something or other, a million miles away in her hospital bed, though knowing, like a knife to a balloon, she'd been vindicated. She finished her Doritos wondering if she could get the airline to pay for her dinner. She fancied a steak. It was the first meal she'd had back from hospital last time. Steak with creamed peas and mash. She'd savoured every bite.

One of the flight staff approached her, a clipboard clutched to her chest, her body slim and efficient in a pencil skirt and heels. They'd booked her a taxi, a hotel and a flight early the next morning. It was time for Jennifer to leave.

She switched on her phone and texted her boyfriend letting him know the situation. You didn't think she had a boyfriend? She did. She always remembered to let him know she'd taken off, always forgot to tell him when she'd landed. She got on her feet. This was her only struggle. She felt like she was forever reaching though her body remained settled and rooted to the ground.

She wondered about the business man. She'd once read that 80% of illnesses don't have a cure. Could a heart run on fumes? Could old lungs forget how to breathe? She took a final look around the hospital waiting room. The doctors and nurses, husbands and wives. She was, she suspected, the most attractive person in the room, in most rooms. She picked up her suitcase and felt a pang in her belly and an ache at her groin. Her period had begun. She waited outside for a long while.

Here's To You

A house seems bigger with nothing in it though nobody mentions the filth.

The dry matter curled in the corners, the sludge below the sink. Without the television and cabinets, the requisite trinkets and knick-knacks, there was little to distract. They had been living like pigs.

Aahna scanned the skirting boards feeling sick, a wretch poised in her throat like a synchronised swimmer, present since the day she was handed her notice.

The kitchenware packed up and shipped off, the DVDs and paperbacks binned. Aahna used to gather and disseminate these things across the local charity shops only to re-accumulate the same old crap over again, her materialism plumping and shedding like the lining of her womb; this, an essential hysterectomy, easy on the hysterics.

She slipped her hand down the side of the couch, the doughy, lumpen mass; once the heaving pivot of their love, the anchor of their alliance, now pushed to the peripheries to gather dust. Grazing the tips of her fingers, she found her bracelet, a tiny gift from her boyfriend, Joyce. She clipped it around her wrist.

He had been alright – he had! – skittish and flapping, a certain buffoon lumber. She remembered when he gave her the bracelet, how he had presented her with it before tea one night, impossibly happy to be sat on the sofa giving her this.

She locked up and posted the keys, heading to the car to move back home. Had things come to this?

They had.

The drive home was tedious. It took twice as long as expected.

Everything seemed to take twice as long as expected. It was as if the whole area were swarming in sleeping sickness.

Hampered with roadworks and the traffic moving sluggishly along. The radiator blasted hot air, a chatty hum emanated off the radio, Aahna started to feel cosy. She yawned and yawned. The little hinges of her jaw chomping up and down. Noticing the last service stop before her turn she pulled in thinking to sink an espresso to nudge her along. She wasn't far now.

Home was one those un-notable Midlands towns. Important, perhaps once, in the early modern era though now known only for mini-breaks and markets. A maze of riveting cobbled streets, of grainy red brick. Autumn crept in like ivy, infusing the place with crackle, with spirit, with a pinching, thrilling cold that swished out your ears and made you pay attention.

The city had two colours; yellow and blue. The light shone either a creamy mayonnaise else it was frosted and navy. Both were oppressive.

At the turn she noticed a blank billboard spray painted over. What do you long for? it asked.

It reminded her of a picture Joyce sent when he'd visited Berlin; Capitalism Kills Love, over a shop front in gaudy neon.

What do you long for?

No EU, came the response, on a yield sign further down the road.

She parked and turned off the engine remaining. As the windows fogged she considered all the romantic notions she'd ever had of herself, multiple identities nurtured and unburdened, free to roam, she supposed, wherever.

She liked the word *wherever*. She liked its shared *e*.

On the radio two biologists talked alternately about the Adriatic Sea and rising tides in Venice. She shut her eyes. She'd never been to Venice. She'd never been to Italy. She'd been abroad once in the past seven years: to Jersey for a wedding.

It was Joyce's cousin and they'd spent most of the evening

getting stoned in the garden. Her resounding memory of the day had been his uncle expressing a deep outrage that they didn't serve tea.

She thought about the wedding; the little lady points of her shoes, how smart Joyce looked in his suit. His uncle smoking outside, saying it was a bastard nuisance it was.

On the radio someone says in Venice water now covers twelve percent of the town.

Aahna was a dancer. Or used to be. She danced here and there, mostly non-professionally; recently with an amateur dramatics group in the chorus line for *The Best Little Whorehouse In Texas*. 'Just a little bitty pissant place,' she sang, breathlessly railing across the stage. 'Ain't nothing much to see!'

Her day job was in audience development at a theatre and dance space; stopping patrons as they left the show, asking whether they'd viewed the performance for 'enrichment, entertainment or as a form of escape?' Sipping tea in the wings she'd stare guilelessly at the small expanse of stage before photocopying proformas on community engagement, typing up risk assessments for cocktail receptions.

'Edible elderflower?!' her manager would scrawl over post-its left on her screen. 'Respond with urgency'.

Lately, she had been dancing less and less. She wasn't sure why. She had something to articulate but didn't have the words. Now, Aahna spent her evenings watching rolling trivia on YouTube; performing small rituals, removing all her make-up and nail varnish, meticulously reapplying with a tiny hand mirror then filing her nails into blunt squares. The less she danced the more she followed a routine.

On her last day at work she sat in the stalls, feet up on the seat in front of her. 'If you've got something to express,' her colleague shouted up in the circle. 'Now is the time.'

She climbed up on stage, delivered an inelegant plié, and skipped to the front.

'My… CUNT!' she yelled, to an audience of one.

'I'm a female artist,' she called up, stepping down. 'What on earth did you expect?'

With Aahna moving back home, Joyce had gone travelling. 'If we're giving up the apartment' he'd reasoned, as if the bricks and mortar of the thing had been all that was holding him back, and Aahna had agreed on the promise of twice daily messages, in the morning and at night. And he would, at obscure times through the day, draft salutations punctuated with a little *x*; the humble aesthetics of the lower-kiss, his circadian rhythms out of whack with hers.

Photos of him with impossibly skinny white girls, in string bikinis and straw hats kept popping up on Facebook; but what could one do? There were goddamn whores the world over.

Aahna stepped into the hallway hearing her mother singing upstairs. A fresh otherworldly remove. A disarming new entropy. Her mother had taken to punctuating melodies with memos. 'Take out the washing,' she'd tell herself after a kicky take on *Summertime*. 'Don't forget to call Sheila.'

Though her mother was dreamy, she was ethereal; the woman was at heart a pragmatist. A wall of good sense against Aahna's drama and histrionics.

Aahna's mother came rattling downstairs, jazzed and made up, lousy with nerves and sweet perfume.

'Bob's taking me out tonight,' she said.

Bob was her mother's boyfriend and he was a disappointment. He was a farmer. Posh and dopey. Always wearing tweed. It's hard to be a disappointment when named Bob. Expectations were already set ludicrously low.

'It's been a terrible year for rape,' he'd told her, the first time they met. 'But the carrots are doing fine.'

She sat in the living room staring at the wall. She'd spent her whole life trying to get out of this place but now whenever she left she had this unnameable melancholy. As she drove past the cornfields, the farmhouses on the outskirts of town, she wasn't sure if she wanted to cry or scream, just a suffocating tug at the centre of her chest.

'Be good, bunny rabbit,' her mother said, kissing her head.

Her high heels delivered an earnest clip clop as she made for the door.

Aahna ate cornflakes for breakfast. Swirling them about the bowl. Peering for meaning within their sodden hieroglyphics. Her mother joined her on the sofa, holding a cup of tea to her breast like an injured bird. She'd gotten in late last night. Aahna was unsure whether Bob had stayed over. It was beyond imagination.

'I hope that's warm milk,' her mother said, peering over.

She had this peculiar obsession with serving everything warm; milk was to be heated before pouring into tea or coffee, water was to be drunk cooled from the kettle. A kind of cushioning against the brutality of the world. What sort of way was it to start the day, anyway, ice cold milk gulped down before stripping naked and showering? Their world was built on small comforts; a benign padding, a benevolent easing in of things.

Aahna nodded and yawned. Last night she had stayed up texting old friends. She smoked some pot before giving up and watching a documentary on the different types of whales. She was done, she thought, with the abstract. What she liked now was the assured. Back in the house, she used to regale Joyce with facts while he'd make them dinner.

No one knows who founded Alcoholics Anonymous. They founded it anonymously.

No one knows who invented the fire hydrant. The patent was burned in a fire.

The singer from The Offspring has his very own line of hot sauce.

She'd stand in front of him like a girl dressed for prom; whaddaya think? He'd pretend to be interested. Deliver a thin smile; all lip flesh and dead eyes. At some point he stopped listening to her facts and talking about where he wanted to visit, his travelling plans that didn't include her. He was in Cambodia now. He'd taken to wearing a leather necklace and thongs. Christ.

Aahna sniffled and picked up the remote. She turned on the television. A programme about agriculture. Unavoidable.

Lying back into the couch she studied her bracelet; the tiny slither of it. She missed Joyce, she supposed, in a distant, misted way. Without him, she felt bored, frustrated.

Sex with Joyce had always been good. Rangey and familiar right from the start. It was like swimming. Afterwards she'd sleep beautifully and wake up starving. Though she didn't so much mind being sexually frustrated. Being a dancer was like being a little bit repressed, always.

Her mother was fussing around the room; pruning the sofa and plumping the pillows.

'When's this audition of yours?' she asked.

Aahna had applied for a job as a nightclub dancer. The requirements of which were some experience and a twenty-six inch waist.

'Tomorrow,' she replied.

It was her first dancing audition in a year. She thought she was through with it. But this felt like being through with it come one step further. Like she'd completed the circle and gone back to the start.

'You know you can always give Bob a hand on the farm.'

Aahna wrinkled her nose. The thought was beyond reproach.

'Suit yourself,' her mother replied. She began humming to herself. Soon would come the memos.

'I ran into your old friend Oliver last week,' she trilled. 'He's just bought a house and I said you'd get in touch.'

Aahna rolled her eyes. 'I'm not sure I'm ready to face the locals,' she said. It was past midday and she was still in her pyjamas. A milk stain shaped like an island. She hadn't washed her hair in days.

'Well think about it,' she said. 'Oliver's got a cat. That can dance.'

She stood up and pointed her toes. Warming up in front of the expansive pastoral scene on the television. She tried moving in time with the chug of a plough, the tractor's dense hum. It was impossible. Capitalism kills love.

'We sound positively made for each other,' she replied, spinning expansively. 'Me and the cat.'

She sat back down. Her mother came and sat next to her, and stroked beneath her chin.

The awful paradox of dancing. The necessary uninhibitedness coupled with the routine appraisal.

Dragging out the ribbons within to be told they're not quite there yet. The hell kind of exoskeletons were dancers equipped with, anyway? How could one flex and jive? The venue was nestled between a model airplane store and a rare books store on the narrow high street. None of the shops here looked like real shops. All prop fronts with nothing inside. Clubs or bars, even chain stores, seemed incongruous; a boom-mic complicating the shot.

Aahna rippled with anxiety. She hated anxiety. Anxiety was a lousy warm-up. She wanted to cut straight to the depression.

Approaching the entrance she thought she recognised some women walking past. Their feet gargantuan in Uggs, twisting St. Christopher chains around their necks. Snow boots and Christians and people you half-knew. You couldn't move for them.

The venue was dark and sticky. She looked for the woman managing the auditions whose name she couldn't remember. The sick familiarity of auditions. Stripping naked and seeing if they're turned on.

'Where can I set up?' she asked.

'Wherever,' the woman replied.

Wherever.

There were about ten girls at the audition, all in varying depths of foundation; their bronzed limbs smoky under the low blue lighting. She watched them shuck and glide, taking their turn upon the stage. She studied their make-up and affectations. All pageantry and no art.

Dancing had started to move her less and less. The first time she'd been to a ballet she'd teared up with an emotion she couldn't really name. Now she counted beats, thought 'bad feet'. Now she felt very little at all. Now when she finished stretching her shoulders ached. Now she could use joint pain to predict the weather.

For the audition she had prepared a short routine. Street dance with a modern flourish. She'd picked a peppy electronic number to back it. Taking to the stage she raised her arms and began.

She flung back her head and hoisted her legs, manipulating her back and shoulders. She popped her joints and bumped her hips. She spun, counting the metre; a rhythmic tick tock to which she buckled and swished.

Express yourself! – she thought. Cunt!

Once, her dance teacher had told her if she was going to make it as a dancer she needed a sense of humour about having no money. 'That's the problem with poverty!' she'd responded. 'No one tells any jokes!' Dancing was all about levity and numbers.

She thrust her body forward, leaping across the stage. She loved the oppressive freedom of dance. The letting go while hanging on. It was dry ryvita and fresh fruit. It was crunches in front of the training mirror. It was bloodied feet and toenails falling off. Equally, it was transformation. She spun beneath the spotlight feeling all the things at once.

As the music slowed she wound down concluding with a diminutive curtsy. Her shoulder throbbed. She'd messed up the end but other than that she hadn't done too bad.

She paused catching her breath. The air was acrid and dank. She felt woozy. A cold panic gripped her throat. Aahna fainted just once before, though felt she understood it. Fainting felt like the correct manifestation of experience.

It had been on holiday after her parents had separated and her mother's settlement came through. They'd gone to Florida. At sixteen, Aahna was a little too old for it; the brightness and pep made her head spin. She felt nauseous constantly, from sugar and corn syrup.

They'd gone to the Epcot Centre which seemed slightly more grown-up, somewhat more sophisticated than the others, though the experience transpired to be singularly nightmarish; plastic and hot, a hellish mesh of caricature and customer satisfaction.

Weaving through the miniature Coliseum, Aahna's vision dimmed and suddenly she was falling to the floor, taking a model Julius Caesar and 3D Mona Lisa with her. Disaster. Drama. Drama in the diorama. 'Aahna!' her mother squealed. 'You brought down Rome!'

As she fell beneath the studio lighting the image remained, along jagged, flickering thoughts, like an ocular migraine. Something about performance. Something about doing what you are told. She woke up to a crowd, to that same garish reminder of vivacity and colour.

A few days before Aahna and Joyce had moved out a pigeon hit the window. They saw it flying straight towards them, clumsy and larger than expected, like a slow-moving albatross. It hit with a thump and fell to the ground. They Googled and rang the RSPCA; became fleetingly, intrepidly fascinated with domestic and feral pigeons. It remained in the yard for hours. They were told birds hitting windows become stunned. It takes them a while to remember how to fly.

They sat cross-legged, urging it to be okay. It strutted and stumbled but eventually flew. It landed on a tree branch on the opposite side of the yard. Another pigeon landed next to it and they nuzzled and cooed; pigeons are monogamous, they mate for life. Aahna and Joyce jumped up and down like giddy schoolgirls, holding each others' hands and squealing with joy. Joyce went to the fridge and opened up a bottle of wine. They toasted on the sofa. 'I am going to be sad when you go,' Aahna thought, and turned on the TV.

It was Halloween and Aahna's mother was cooking. She was making pumpkin dahl. Kneading lantern-orange flesh with sage. Warming spices over the stove. Aahna had persuaded her mother to watch *The Red Shoes* with her.

'It doesn't seem very Halloween-y,' she said.

'Trust me,' Aahna replied. 'It's terrifying.'

Aahna opened a bottle of wine and they both stood drinking it in the kitchen. Aahna was beginning to enjoy being at home. There were always biscuits in the cupboard, fresh towels on the rack. She was increasingly seeing herself through her mother's eyes; had started dressing in brighter, more fragrant colours.

Trick-or-treaters gathered at the front door. Aahna spied them through the kitchen window: Madonna, Cher and Tina. Divas-in-training. Pre-divas. Hunched together in nylon costumes.

They looked strange in grown-up clothes. All youthful sass and bad posture.

'Do you like Chardonnay?' Aahna asked.

She held her glass in the air. Here's to you! She was drunk.

The flimsy sequins of their costumes twinkled nervously in the dark. Red toenails peeping self-consciously from their sandals. They popped their hips. Smacked their glossed lips.

Aahna looked them up and down. Bitches, she thought. Bitches.

'You look more like Pinot girls, am I right ladies?'

She held their gaze.

'You want to see a trick?' Madonna asked, and then she spat on the floor. They screamed with laughter and turned to run away. They tripped and fell into each other, hysterical and squealing. Children are awful.

'Hey, that's not very polite,' Aahna shouted after them. 'That's not very fucking Mother of Jesus.'

The clip clop of their heels echoed down the street. They whooped with glee.

'Cher,' Aahna shouted after them.

'Hey Cher. I've got a question for you.'

They stopped, breathless. Holding onto each other. They turned around and their eyes shimmered with expectation.

'Oh yeah,' Cher replied.

'Yeah,' Aahna shouted.

'Do you believe in life after love?'

The girls looked at each other in disbelief. They giggled, giddy and drunk; drunk on this crazy lady, scampering back down the street like wild things into the night.

'Well do you?' Aahna yelled after them.

'Do you?'

Aahna closed the door and went back inside. Her mother was laying the table.

'Am I a good person?' Aahan asked.

'Hmm?'

'Am I a good person?' she repeated.

Her mother patted her head.

'Good at what?' she asked.

At her mother's insistence Aahna had agreed to meet her old schoolfriend Oliver. She needed to get out the house. Skyping with Joyce, she had so little to report; 'my IBS is back' and 'Aldi do kale now' while his anecdotes were conspicuously littered with vowel-heavy girls' names, a new drag in his voice dense with overstimulated inertia.

He Snapchatted her a picture of a Buddhist temple and another of his feet in the sand. She'd stared at them listlessly counting down the seconds. Good riddance, she'd think, as they vanished.

Oliver had offered to cook her dinner. Her mother dropped her off. She paused outside his house arrested by the sight of it; a proper little house, stucco exterior, porch light and a neatly manicured lawn. It looked like a cartoon house. Phantasmagorically domestic. Too good to be true.

They hovered in the kitchen nervously catching up on their respective lives. Oliver worked for a pneumatics company ('the pressure gets a bit much'), still said 'ace' a lot. It was weird seeing his schoolboy face grown old. Like a practical joke. Like he might kick her in the shins and tell his friends she believed him.

'Your pal Stephen once asked me out,' Aahna said. 'As a joke.'

'Did he?' Oliver replied.

'Yes. And before I could answer he said 'I just remembered I'm gay'. I wasn't even going to say yes.'

'Sure you weren't.'

'Funny thing is – now he is. Now he is gay.'

'Funny old world, huh?'

'I ran into him in Liverpool. He called his boyfriend 'little earwig'. You can precede almost anything with little and make it sound affectionate. Little scarab. Little human centipede.'

'Little chum.'

'Good one.'

They sat down for dinner. As Aahna surveyed the table she realised, not with horror, or happiness, more with a sort of unbiased anthropological curiosity, that the evening was a date.

It was a strange date for people who didn't date. A date learned from movies, moist with cliché, sloppy with pre-packaged cannelloni. She prodded them with her spoon; sad, wet tubes oozing green goo, blanketed by a sickly tomato sauce.

Desert was scooped out of plastic cups with what looked like a half-peeled reduced sticker clinging to their side. But the carefully arranged napkins and recently hoovered carpet told her the evening was not without thought, without occasion, at least not to him and she felt a pang of – was it tenderness? she supposed, a certain winning over, staring at his badly ironed shirt, a crisp, pink shirt, he clearly thought himself rather radical, rather on-the-nose in, though if pushed, would doubtlessly decree the shirt salmon, a salmon shirt; the colour of flesh, of muscle, of the outdoors.

The famed cat, the performer, the warm-up act, was sleeping in the kitchen, making an appearance as Aahna polished off her fourth glass of wine.

'I hear he dances,' she said, scratching the top of his head.

'Oh yes,' replied Oliver, turning up the music, kneeling on the floor, holding his paws and waltzing him across the living room floor.

'He's called Kitty,' he said, setting the cat on her knee.

Aahna stroked the soft velvet beneath his chin as he jutted forward his jaw; where did cats learn to be so forward? – to the right a bit, there, yes, harder. He had black patches across his eyes, and dipped black socks, but was otherwise white all over.

'He looks more like a little panda than a cat,' she said, lifting him up.

'Oh Kitty,' she leered, his body contorting in a stiff C. A rigid crescent moon.

'Kitty! Kitty! Kitty! We all want more than our god given bodies!'

She placed him back down on the floor, feeling a strange generosity, a peculiar magnanimity and when her taxi arrived and Oliver walked her to the door, pressing his mouth slightly to the side of hers, she leaned in, and in the spirit of giving and gravity, reciprocated, whispering for him to send the taxi away.

Aahna woke to the dry expanse of an empty bed. She stared at the ceiling, the grooved pattern of the tiling as comforting and uncannily familiar as the tinkering downstairs. The strange and disorienting joy of being the second person awake. She stretched out, making lazy snow angels in the sheets, luridly monopolising the bed. Pulling the full weight of the duvet across her. Being alone was its most glorious when there was someone else around.

She rolled onto her stomach and considered brushing her teeth. Her eyeliner stained the pillowcase and her hair was dry as a sponge. It had been a while since she'd idled about a kitchen in an oversized t-shirt languidly eating toast.

She collected her various items of clothing dotted around the room, found her underwear folded neatly on the dresser. Her head hurt. She felt hungry and morose; a little bit sick.

In the kitchen Oliver was cooking. He poured her a fresh cup of coffee. He kissed her forehead and remarked she was 'a vision'. She was inclined to agree.

In the cold light of day she wandered around downstairs. It was such a clean house. No dust on the sides. No hair on the carpet. How did one maintain it? What even was the point? She lingered in the hallway sipping her coffee. On the bookshelf she noticed a book of facts. She picked it up and flicked through the pages.

Thread count is a myth.

Cows have accents.

Alazia is the fear that you are no longer able to change.

She dropped it to the floor. She felt dizzy. Lightheaded. Warm. The room began suddenly to spin. She felt her way to the front door. Went outside for some fresh air.

Outside, she sat in the grass. The tightly cropped lawn all dewy from the morning. Its soft solidity felt certain and assured. Her bottom felt wet and muddy. This, she thought. There is only this.

She had wanted sand but she had gotten soil. It had its benefits, sure. You put something in the earth and out comes something else. How can you wrangle with the oblivion of a lazy ocean, with the saltwater crack of the wind. No wonder farmers were so arrogant. Cats so forthright.

She half stood-up, resting on the backs of her heels. She thought about going back in but a stoic disinclination to move, to go anywhere, rendered her incapable. The air was cool. The road wasn't too busy. Oliver was calling her name.

She looked out onto the horizon, breathing steadily; breathing from her stomach, from her groin. The dense theatrics of the skyline. The woozy promise of the road. It seemed she could be wherever. An *e* caught between two extremes.

What do you long for?

She didn't know what she wanted and she never had; her wants extended everywhere, inside and out, up and down; an undulating blob of non-specific desire.

What the hell did she want? What did anyone?

'Aahna!'

Breakfast was ready and the carpet was clean. There were worse things in this world. She sighed the long sigh of a life of never quite being enough.

'Aahna,' Oliver yelled. 'Are you coming back inside?'

She got on her feet.

She was.

Sundaes At The Tipping Yard

Begin a Creative Writing MA punctuating a long, lazy summer. You've quit your job, your flat, your boyfriend. Your life feels like a pot left too long on the hob; the lid removed revealing the calcified remains of before. Chew the end of a pencil's gummy eraser. Twirl hair around your finger. You are grace under fire. You are one of the gals from *Grease*.

But the MA is the thing. You have trundled towards it for a long while now and here it is; lolling and mewing in your lap. Do it right. Buy subject dividers from Amazon. There will be books and workshops and debates on the demise of the publishing industry in the wake of digitalisation. Wear a leather satchel and paint your nails. Make caustic notes in your Moleskine. Tell them you like Nabokov. Look at your reading list and buy only the women.

In preparation you start writing. You start really writing. At night you throw up; throwing up your guts, your thoughts, your darkest and most shameful feelings, arranging them on the page in a way you find pleasing. You also throw up because you have an eating disorder. It comes and goes. It hitches to what it can. Knock back 20 milligrams of diazepam with a tepid glass of white wine. It is in these moments and these moments alone you feel like a writer.

You meet your classmates; they are bankers, lawyers, caretakers; they work for restaurants, call centres, nautical engineering firms. No one owns a Kindle but everyone has a Mac. There is a lot of knitwear. You are all very concerned about the demise of the publishing industry in the wake of digitalisation. Sit at the back of the room. When asked what you think, reply: 'I'm sorry, what?' After class everyone will cycle home.

You need somewhere new to live. Somewhere cheaper. Somewhere that is not your friend Margot's cat hair-covered couch. You view a loft conversion in town; five minutes to the cinema, ten minutes to everything else. There is a large sombrero on the living room floor. The live-in landlord, Chuck, puts it on and points at his head. 'I think this,' he says, 'tells you everything you need to know about me.' He shows you the room. 'Most weekends,' he tells you, 'I have twenty or so mates around and we stay up partying for days. Is this going to be a problem?' This is going to be a problem. This is objectively going to be a problem. 'This is not going to be a problem,' you say. You take the room.

You have your first story to workshop. It is a story about rape. Reading it, you are distracted. You would like to watch *The Simpsons*. You would like to bake rosemary and sea salt bread. You think maybe you could learn Dreamweaver off YouTube. You were supposed to be more engaged. 'Nothing,' you recall telling your ex-boyfriend, stamping your stiletto, spoiled as spoiled Veruca Salt, blue on blueberry pie, 'nothing is more important than this.' You sigh and turn the page. You sign in to Twitter.

The leaves turn and suddenly it is autumn. Dense and operatic; the most eloquent of seasons. It is a time for women. It is a time for melancholy. It is a time for knocking back 20 milligrams of diazepam with a tepid glass of white wine. Wear ankle boots to the park. A pea coat and a plum coloured beret. Notice the air. Spend time thinking about air. Eat only tomato soup for a week.

Your mind keeps turning to your ex; your old brown shoe. One night you accidentally like one of his girlfriend's photographs on Instagram. You send him an email telling him you have not lost your mind though quite evidently you have. He does not reply. There are no accidents, rattles through your brain. There are no accidents. Did Freud say that? Or Cher?

Chuck is bored, sleepy. Hanging around the kitchen and

making oven food. Talking about his old roommate, Mindy. He wants to have a beer. He always wants to have a beer. You sit opposite each other and try to think of things to talk about. He tells you he loves films. He's gaga for them. He is a bona fide film buff. 'What's your favourite film?' you ask, disinterestedly. He stares out of the window for a long while. 'I'd have to say,' he replies, 'Finding Nemo.'

In class you discuss the story. The one about rape. 'Rape is about power,' you take turns saying, sagely. After class you go for drinks and the story writer tells you she is an alcoholic. You tell her your father left when you were five. 'Oh, that's awful,' she replies. 'It wasn't so bad,' you say. 'He came straight back. He'd just gone to the store.'

At night you wander the flat; roaming from room to room like a listless spectre. You check the doors are locked. You eat cereal feverishly over the sink. Chuck keeps checking up on you. The cord of his dressing gown hanging limp from his waist like a sad umbilical cord.

Your tutor tells you there are choices to be made; and are there ever! Choose a wild boy who will rip out your heart or a nice boy of whom you will grow tired. It hardly matters. It all ends with the same miserable solitude. But he means more to do with your essay; have you picked a question yet?

Chuck has made tacos. He would like you to have a taco night. 'Mindy loved tacos,' he says, piling on guacamole. 'And musicals!' He watches you tap at your laptop taco in hand. 'You know,' he says. 'You can't teach writing.' You pretend not to hear. After you're done eating you disappear to the bathroom for an hour.

You begin meeting boys off the internet. One who is writing a graphic novel. Another who works at a record store. Another doing a postdoctoral on neoliberalism in the early episodes of *Seinfeld*. They all labour how much they do not want to have a relationship with you and none of them listen to anything you have to say. 'You might as well leave,' you say, watching them put on their clothes. 'You might as well leave before I throw up.'

You need a job. Your money is running out and your cereal is running low. You send out your CV to offices, bars, to telesales call centres on the outskirts of town. You get an interview as a product review writer. The call comes after class while you lie outside thinking about the uncanny. 'I wasn't expecting this,' you say, though, perhaps you were? Buy a smart skirt. Wear it once on your first day, spill tomato soup over it and so, never again. There are no accidents, sings Cher.

You write some short fiction for workshop. It is about a girl who quits her job, her boyfriend, her flat and does a Creative Writing MA. It is the first time you have read in front of your class. A bit like losing your virginity you feel more or less the same, but you would like to have a bath. 'How about,' your tutor suggests, 'you write a story that's not about your ex-boyfriend?' You go home and write a story you are sure is not about your ex-boyfriend, one about a mermaid living in Queens; a mermaid who quits her job, her boyfriend, her flat and starts a Creative Writing MA. 'You can't make these things up!' you scribble in the margins. You literally cannot make these things up.

You bite your lip one night eating tacos. You study its surface. Its bulbous, fleshy tumour. Chuck offers you a margarita. You sip it, peeling back your mouth to stop it from hurting. Chuck lifts up your drink and places it on a coaster. 'Sometimes,' he says, 'I wonder if you were born in a barn.'

In class you have discussions, you ask important questions. Are you showing or telling? Have you overqualified this verb? Can you form a meaningful relationship online? Has anyone ever met a psychopath? There are so many dead girls. Everyone supposes everything is a metaphor for sperm. Think: you are honing your skills. Think: Sundaes At The Tipping Yard is a pretty good name for a bestseller.

You meet another boy off the internet. You both like books so you sleep with him. In the morning he says that you look like a deer. Somewhere, in the thickets, something is shifting.

Chuck has taken to perching on your bed drinking coffee in the mornings. 'Mindy was supposed to come round tonight,' he says. 'But now she can't make it.' He lies down; splayed at your ankles like Christ. It occurs to you that Chuck is in love with Mindy. That his heart is breaking, slowly. You pat his shoulder. 'There there,' you say. 'There there, mate.'

You catch up with your friend Elle after work. She is a nurse at a cancer hospital. You tell her you've had a terrible day. That you spilled milk everywhere and then your boss was unpleasant. She tells you she's had a terrible day. That a patient died and now she's worried she's going to be sued. You order cocktails and get very drunk. She tells you in hospitals they call the mortuary "the Rose Garden". Think: that is so sad. Think: you could use that in a story. Your lip remains half-eaten, swollen.

You write your essay. You write your essay on the story about rape. You re-read it carefully. Re-reading it many times. Rape, you think. Is about power.

This new boy wants you to do magic mushrooms while bowling. You get three strikes giggling wildly. You order chips but can't eat a thing. Walking home he tells you the names of all the trees. You press your face into his shoulder and it smells of salt. You hold hands all the way to your door.

You present your last piece at workshop. Your class like it. You have an improved sense of character, a fresh and economic voice. It is not about your ex-boyfriend. Though none of this matters as Raymond Carver has already written this particular story, it's in his collection *Will You Please Be Quiet Please* which, you don't say, you have not read.

Bummer.

Your first term is over and you didn't do so bad. You would like to celebrate. You have a new flat, a new job, a new boyfriend. You are doing a Creative Writing MA. You book a table for two. You say it is your treat.

You order the tasting menu. Celeriac and kale salad. Gnocchi and beer-battered halloumi. Gin and tonic sponge cake. It costs you a fortune. You toast. You toast to your new job. To your MA. To your boyfriend. Your dreamy new boyfriend! You finish your drink in one. 'Babe,' he says. 'I think we need to agree on a vocabulary.'

You come home crying. Chuck is watching television with an empty bottle of wine.

'I got dumped,' you say.

'Mindy's engaged,' he replies.

You sit and notice the air.

'It's an education,' you tell him, apropos of nothing. 'It's all an education.'

You lie facing Chuck on the opposite settee. You think about how things become faint. That one day you will squint back upon a time when the selfie stick was considered absurd. Writing cannot be taught. Rape is about power. Sundaes At The Tipping Yard is a pretty good name for a bestseller. Tongue the bitten part of your lip. It is flat and smooth. It is still sore.

Are you showing or telling? It is hard to say. There are things to be learned and there are things to be felt and occasionally the two overlap; and that's where the trouble begins.

'Education?' Chuck says, drunk and bloated, beached on the sofa. 'More like, edu – lame! – tion.'

Badabing!

Is he right?

It is likely, you suppose, staring at the star shaped capillaries expanding around his eyes. It is quite likely he is not wrong.

Safe Spaces

I have started meditating. I go to classes twice a week. I remove my shoes and ball up my socks. I tuck them into the soles before slipping them within the wire lockers available for our convenience. I smile at the other meditators but I do not make chit-chat. That is not why we're here. The cushions and stools are stacked at the right corner of the room. I sit at the left corner of the room. On my first session I sat on the stool with my legs wedged either side of it and the stool was too short to fully support my weight so I more or less squatted my legs holding my weight for the first fifteen minutes of breathing exercises shaking and burning and hurting a lot. I bit my lip to distract myself from the pain. When the instructor asked if there were any questions I replied yes what's everyone doing later just so I would have the chance to sort of moan and he said he meant more to do with meditation but since I asked he was going for a drink and we were all welcome to join him. He placed his hand on my back to show me how to breathe correctly. The tip of his fingernail sliding beneath the top of my underwear just the tip pulling back the stringy white elastic pressed against the braille of my skin. A perfect white arc of fingernail.

I have started taking baths. Baths I have realised are for when you do not have anyone to hold. I remove my clothes in the bedroom and walk naked down the hall into the bathroom. It's not that I like or feel comfortable with my body it's just that it's there it is something that I'm dealing with. I sink into the bathwater my breasts bob in the bubbles ridiculous round things really carrying them about with you like a gaudy tea tray jelly in the trunk. The shower head hangs over me like a flat round disk like something you'd see on a spaceship on television. I think about switching it on flipping back the tap with my toes letting the water run over me like rainfall but then he rings and I answer and he says he's coming in an hour if I'm free which he knows right well I will be. I get out of the bath and walk through to the living room my steps heavy and graceless feeling a little drunk bath drunk not alcohol drunk. I don't drink anymore not after last time with the vodka and the Bat Mitzvah and that little girl crying saying she's been sick she's been sick everywhere she's been sick in the punch and me having to leave without giving her my present. He arrives an hour later and I am still wrapped in my bath towel and he says this is good this is how you should always dress untucking the top corner and I spin around unwrapping myself like a dancer and we make love on the sofa and he strokes my hair for five or ten minutes.

I have started going to cafés. Just one café really if I am going to be completely straightforward. I always order a vanilla latte and a banana nut muffin because I saw that on TV once and it seemed like a sophisticated combination though truth be told it is a little sickly for my liking. I sit by the window and take out my book and look like I'm reading thinking this is when I'll frown a bit this is when I'll turn over the page. I eat my muffin tearing it into sections nibbling it bit by bit. Last time I tore into my muffin I could see all these fibrous things that on closer inspection I realised must be insects. Spiders I suspect. Ground up and baked into the mix. I took a small piece of muffin wrapped it in a napkin and showed the waiter asking what the meaning of all these spiders was and he said there were no spiders and gave me a funny look and then I looked around and all the other customers were giving me funny looks too though not half as funny as the looks they gave me when he walked in with her with his wife and I called her a bitch whore and asked quite reasonably why she couldn't keep her man pleased you know in a sexual sense throwing the last of my muffin at her spilling coffee all down myself then leaving without looking at him but knowing I'd probably have to find somewhere else to meditate.

I have started taking walks. I walk alone at night the sky looks nice all theatrical and old like a heavy curtain of velvet that would catch you and land you softly in it if for whatever reason the world turned upside down and you fell. I pull back my hair into a ponytail and pull it tightly to smooth the wrinkles across my forehead. I don't have many wrinkles if I am to be honest and the night sky is not unkind to them. I walk up past the park and then round past the playground the primary colours gone inky by the dark like somebody spilled black paint into all the other colours. I used to think walks like baths like meditation were a pointless liturgy however now I see their appeal the silken comfort of the retreat the sedate charm of the remove. I look at the windows and think about the people in them thinking this one's maybe a botanist this one has bad luck this one's got a hard life this one lost his wife and now he can't get out of bed in the morning. Once on my way home I walked past him and he said what the hell are you doing here what the hell are you even doing out here and I said I was out on my stroll I was just out on my evening stroll.

I have started a new meditation class. It is further away than the other at the Buddhism centre in town but the instructor is nice with a pale moon face and a smooth shaved head and when you get down to it this is the sort of thing Buddhists excel in. I tried a few others before I found this one but what I found is they're mostly the same the same people the same breathing the same absent groaning wanting; a safe space they say imagine a safe space they always say your paradise your dream desert island but for all my imagining for all my thoughts drifting moonwards up; up into the soupy wash of sky up into the fluffy white cotton clouds up into the star speckled universe. Just an infinitesimal pinprick moving further and further away.

A Single Lady's Manual for Parent/
Teacher Evening

A whistling nebula of Optrex and espresso, of barely
contained hysteria, you arrive late, smoothing your wool skirt,
plucking bobbles from your cardigan. Your hair swishes in a
high ponytail, a slack whip, grazing your neck and shoulders,
your horn-rimmed glasses kick queasy angles above your
cheeks. You remove a wasabi pea from a crackling packet
within your coat pocket. You slip it into your mouth chewing
with a precision that makes you feel capable and wise. You're
concerned no one here really – gets – your outfit. You're
concerned maybe they don't read *Cosmo.*

'Your husband couldn't make it?' asks his Geography
teacher. You have built armour for this. It props you up like
scaffolding. 'I don't have a husband,' you say. 'It's just me.'
You look him in the eye. You look him hard in the eye. A thin
whisper of grey splinters his forehead, a crease of skin, like a
loose sock, sags at the curve of his nose. Your move, you think.
Your move, asshole.

You look at the other mothers, you see how they regard
you, a sinister rogue agent, with small, sharp teeth and a face
full of make-up. They grip their husbands. You wish you were
wearing something lower cut.

His English teacher clears her throat, shuffling papers
across the table. 'He doesn't talk much,' she says. 'He's a very
quiet boy.' You look at him and think: Quiet? This gangly,
leaping thing. This giant bratty creature, preponderating your
house, bounding across the living room, as playful as a kitten.
Quiet? 'Wasabi pea?' you ask.

You wander through to the Art studios. You nod to a
student in a cravat and beret. 'Got ourselves a real David

Hockney,' you nudge your son. 'I said, we've got ourselves a real David Hockney, if you know what I mean.' He wrinkles his face. 'What are you talking about?' he says. 'Also, you have lipstick on your teeth. You have lipstick literally all over your teeth.'

You recognise a boy with a strained, scattered beard. You study its lazy cartography. He used to visit your house. You smile at him. 'Isn't that Christian?' you ask, nodding in his direction. 'Aren't you going to say hello?' He mumbles something, staring at his feet, scratching his chin. 'Speak up,' you say. 'Speak up. I can't hear a word you're saying.'

You are hot – too hot – in the science labs. You remove your coat, ripping it from your arms, he holds your purse and scarf as you fan yourself wildly. A group of young men walk by, giggling and chatting, as involved as Christmas elves. They see him holding your bag, your quilted bag, with its glossy oversized clasp and your printed silk scarf. 'Oh Matilda!' they laugh. 'Look at what Matilda's holding!' He forces them back into your hands. 'Come on,' he says. 'Come on, we're going.'

'He is a bright kid,' his Biology teacher tells you. 'He is just as bright as a button.' You look at him, you look at his face, his big dopey face, the light of it, the captured, amber light. Light that needs splitting and refracting to burn even brighter. You want to hold his hand. You think if you were to hold his hand, at this moment in time, you would break every bone in it, crushing them down to sawdust.

You cross the playground, looping an arm through his. 'What are you doing this weekend, pal? Why don't you go to the cinema?' You slip him a twenty pound note. 'My treat.' He yawns, removing his arm from yours. 'I thought I'd just hang out with you this weekend,' he says. 'Plus the dishwasher isn't going to fix itself.' Last night, he made you a lasagne, looming in the arched entrance of your kitchen, in your rose print apron and oven gloves. 'You are so handsome,' you say, squeezing his cheek with your thumb and forefinger. 'You are such a handsome boy.'

You meet his final teacher of the evening, his Media Studies teacher, she is about your age. 'I work in Digital Marketing,' you tell her. 'But I did a Masters in Film and Media years and years ago.'

'Well it must run in the family,' she replies. 'Because he is doing fantastic.' You give his wrist a little squeeze. His tiny, baby wrist. 'His project on Jean Seberg,' she says, 'is really excellent work.'

'He did a project on Jean Seberg?' you reply, turning to him. 'Did you really? My dissertation was on Jean Seberg.'

'I know,' he says. 'You told me.'

'Well,' his teacher says. 'You must read his project. The stuff about her poetry is particularly interesting.'

'She wrote poetry? No kidding,' you say. 'I didn't know.'

You drum your fingers on the table and look at your watch. How did I not know that? you think. How on earth did I not know that? You thought you knew everything about Jean Seberg. You thought you could write the goddamn book on Jean Seberg.

You look at your boy. Well, perhaps it is new information, you think, freshly acquired knowledge you are not privy to, something you simply do not have time to keep on top of. Or perhaps you once knew, and now you have forgotten, stowing it away, treading water between the bleeding multitude of things you have to think about. Or perhaps you knew all along, and you have overlooked it. Or is it possible, is it just possible, that you never knew.

Not really.

Not even at all.

A Selfie As Big As The Ritz

After the Faculty party Samuel held her sensing somehow she was different.

Her body felt unusually hard; a stiff little nub, defiant in its rigidity, whereas before it felt soft and expansive, as smooth and yielding as down. He suddenly saw its capacity for secrets. The scoop of her hips. The spaces between the vertebrae of her spine. He slipped a hand beneath her breast. You could hide a twenty pence piece under here, he thought. You could hide a fifty pound note!

She had worn a silver dress; a slinky, rustling number, shining like some tinfoil covered treat. There was an arrogance in silver, he felt. A false modesty. Second best! How terribly humble! He watched her move across the room, stacking salad and samosas onto her plate, shimmering like some other-worldly thing, something dimensionally beyond his reach. He suddenly understood the movie *Ghost*. He thought: that's actually an incredibly profound film.

Now that the cartography of her body no longer made sense, like a map written in verse, nothing else seemed to make sense also. He doubted whether he had ever known her at all. She had started drifting. She drifted backwards and forwards. She drifted from one room to another. 'The drift!' he'd exclaim, but she frowned and shrugged her shoulders. She no longer understood his references.

He surveyed the room; the huddled modernists, the distended narratologists, the Americanists being loud and brash (of course). Standing together in groups of twos, threes and fives; a couple of loners circling the room. A chaotic Fibonacci sequence! he thought, with her at the centre of all things in a way he had never really noticed, dressed like a precious metal.

He normally enjoyed these Faculty hubbubs. He was a sharp dresser. A sophisticated fella. But he was preoccupied. She seemed more angular, more disengaged than usual. All sloping curves and smooth skin. There was no getting past beautiful women, you just sort of buzzed about their peripheries; hanging around the front door, waiting for an invite inside.

He found himself following her, draping his arm around her neck, wanting to throw a tantrum, a full spitting tantrum, just so she would look at him. Though sex remained the same. She still wanted him in this final, absolute sense. Staring into her eyes he could see that same hunger, that same aching blue oblivion. After, he would draw his fingertip around the outline of her face and she would shiver, though not, he knew, from pleasure.

Watching her sleep he decided what they needed was something to make them fall in love again: a shared interest in lomography, or a really good boxset. She had recently taken an interest, her own private interest, in environmental politics. She'd inherited an esoteric vernacular as if intentionally to exclude him. Phrases like 'crop phrenology' and 'intraspecific diversity' she would intone with the depth of prayer. She started clipping articles from the paper and taping them to their bedroom wall. The frantic collaging of the deranged. He would return from work, observe her supine on the sofa, like some undersexed Victorian, then wearily climb the stairs, peeling the clippings carefully and placing them in a black plastic bag to bin.

He tried to ingratiate himself to this interest; reading up on ecopoetics, delivering articulate meditations on pastoralism over dinner. He imagined he must look very attractive to her, like that Athena poster of the man holding the baby. He paused, occasionally, to ask her views, and she just smiled and rocked forward her head. He thought it was probably a lot to take in.

Holding her at night he smiled. Smiled for the small victories. The hamlets torched. The villagers mutely ravaged. The towns and cities far, far away. They were, after all, still fucking.

Sometimes he got the sense he could do anything to her and that she would like it. He removed the rather unpleasant thought, like hair from the drain, replacing it with the notion that he should whisk her away. He imagined her in that silver dress, glittering like a disco ball. Beneath the freshly acquired layers of hemp wool and patchouli remained the heart of a glamourpuss, he mustn't forget that. He would razzle dazzle her. Sweep her off her feet. Take her to Paris for a weekend of romance and roses.

On the flight she listened to country music – a clear indication of melancholy.

It was lazy. It was lazy heartbreak. Resigning yourself to strings and lazy metaphors, empty ballrooms and birthday parties no one shows up for. It lacked fight. For what were the heart's aches and pains if not a call to arms? He had the stewardess bring them a bottle of champagne but it just made her sad. He gave her a playlist of all his favourite songs but she didn't want to listen. Was there nothing he could do?

Though she did seem to like the hotel. She flopped immediately onto the bed and wrapped herself in the duvet, like a plump sausage roll, her head peeping out at the end. He kissed her, holding her soft halo in his hands. 'You look good today,' he said, and she blinked, twice, though didn't return the gesture.

He had the whole weekend planned. A river boat up the Seine, a walk around the Sorbonne; they would hold hands and visit graves. He would duck into little patisseries to buy her treats but she would eat them with a perfunctory grazing. He wondered why she hadn't dressed with a little more whimsy. Why she would not say anything, merely stare off into space. Was there ever anything more terrifying than other people's thoughts?

Approaching the Eiffel Tower he implored her to hold her hand skyward, a perspective photo; looking as if it were placed in her palm. She refused, shaking her head, letting all her hair fall into her eyes like the limp tassels on one of the imitation designer handbags she wouldn't let him buy. At the top of the tower, she would still not have her photograph taken, and hadn't offered to take his. He angled the phone in front of his face, the screen beaming back his reflection. He thought he looked very handsome today. Well, it would be a fantastic selfie. A magnificent selfie. A selfie as big as the Ritz.

She left soon after they returned. There was no decisive moment; she just sort of faded away. One day he looked around the flat and realised none of the stuff in it was hers. It was a relief really; the sleepy calm that comes after the exorcism of grief. And so, he slept it off. Slept like slowly seeping caramel. Slept like the biggest marshmallow there ever was. He didn't so much mind his life without her.

Some months later he saw her in the supermarket, in a stained shirt and clogs; a string bag of limes in one hand, box of tampons in the other. He thought he might go over and see if she was okay, ask how she was doing; but there was something about how she looked that made him pause. She looked still as if she was drifting. She looked confused. She looked like, maybe, she had been crying. He followed her for a long while, wandering through the aisles, beginning to approach her then pulling back; watching her drop things and get herself into a state. At one point, she turned and almost saw him, but he ducked behind some crackers, kneeling low on the floor; wondering what he was supposed to do or say, wondering if she'd ever even seen him at all.

The Getting Of the Cat

There is a going-into-things-with-your-eyes-open, in the getting of the cat. It is a buying into a specific kind of identity. An identity of Blossom Dearie glasses; of chrome-plated reading lamps. Of a copy of *The Fountainhead* splayed open, text forward, like a yawn, the spine cracked and wrinkled, the pages sticky with thumbprints. It is a decision you make not without understanding the implications, indeed, without embracing them, and so it was fitting the cat was collected on your birthday, an indifferent gift to yourself, a nonchalant scarf or dispassionate tea set, that gleams and spits from the corner.

You step outside into the shared garden of your flat, in the warehouse district, where your friends used to live, though they have moved to the suburbs, to settle down, to tend allotments and complain about the lack of adequate cycle routes.

You really need this cat.

You can hold it in your arms and waltz it around the garden, the pretty periwinkles in their red, brick beds, the slanted paving and sad water feature, water sort of spewing from its side, like an epileptic tongue. You can show your cat all of this, scratching the silken fuzz of his head, holding its warm paw in the palm of your hand. 'This is it,' you can say. 'This is outside.'

You collect it from the shelter, arriving midday, greeted by the woman you have spoken with, Ellen, in tartan tights, berry nail varnish and whispering, silver hair. Watercolour paintings hang limp from the walls. A potted plant wilts on the table, its leaves spilling over the side, in deference. Ellen looks at you like she recognises you as One Of Us, which of course you are; a cat person, allies in isolation. 'He's had a sleepless night,' she says, placing him on the table in a creaking, wicker basket. He cowers at the back, his emerald eyes, like lilies on a lake, bob and float from the shadows.

You carry him out like a proud purchase, a chiffon shirt from a ritzy store, in a meringue paper bag, finished with a wide satin bow. You set him on the passenger seat and he begins to purr; a bottomless animal hum, drowned as you switch on the engine.

You run into Mrs. Kowalski in the hall and she holds the door open for you. 'I've got a cat,' you say, lifting the basket towards her. 'I can see that,' she replies. 'Oh, I can see that.' She looks you up and down, pursing her lips together, her lipstick cracking into spidery ducts.

You release him into the bedroom, he slips vaporously from his basket, navigating the boundaries of the room. 'Here kitty,' you call, dangling a felt bell. 'Here, kitty, kitty, kitty.' He sniffs the bell and turns from you, slowly, hopping onto the bed and sitting down, with a calculation you can only describe as sociopathic.

His name comes to you as a complete and indisputable truth; just popping in your brain one morning, like a balloon. Hank. His name is Hank.

You find to your dismay that Hank is a licker. There is something unpleasantly insipid, something uncharacteristically pandering, about a cat that licks. You extend your hand as he laps conscientiously at it, looking up for your approval. You feed him only tinned fish; mackerel in tomato sauce, sardines in olive oil; after the peculiar philosophy Do Not Feed Him What You Yourself Would Not Eat, occurs to you, as clear and as certain as a shard of glass. You scoop salmon from the can, breaking it up with the side of your fork, and watch the grey pink flesh scatter and ooze.

Hank is a big cat. You had not anticipated such a big cat. You feel like you are sharing your home with a beast roaming wild across your living room, all id, jumping on furniture, forcing his face into your food. Last Wednesday, he defecated into your hand, he literally defecated into your hand. Oh! – but he looked so embarrassed afterwards! His little tail down, like a limp paintbrush, swirling steady circles around his bowl. You would forgive him anything. You understand people who have cats that walk all over their babies, why they let them do it, I mean, who are they hurting, really?

You have a date. You are finished going out for dates, now you have them in. You have them in your flat; these are my insides, do you like what you see? He is late but he has brought wine. You turn on the radio. Hank loiters at the door in uncertain investigation. You have cooked dinner; scrambled egg, grilled peppers and a dollop of mashed potatoes. 'This is a really weird dinner,' he says.

He fetches more wine from the kitchen, pulling open the drawers, searching for the bottle opener. You follow him in, forcing your hands down the back of his trousers, just to see if you can, removing them swiftly. 'Can I get you some dessert?' you ask, thinking whether you could leave, whether you could just feasibly leave, come back in a few hours, and hope that he has gone.

You sit on the couch. 'I had a cat when I was a kid,' he says. 'Did you ever have a cat when you were little?'

You did. You did have a cat. Your mother gave you a cat for your birthday, a few weeks before she left. It was a fragile cat, a cat on borrowed time, with brittle bones and fur sprouted in patches, as though it was only just managing to be there at all. It didn't live much longer after she had gone. You wept when it died, which is perhaps strange, as you didn't particularly like this cat; the dopamine trance of its stare, its hesitant way of creeping onto your lap. You let it out one morning, and while sipping from a cup of tea, an amber calm descended, and you understood it wouldn't be coming back. And you cried.

Hank hops onto the couch and you cup his face in your hands, touching his cold, wet nose with your own. Your date sighs. 'What is it with women and cats?' he asks.

Your mother was very catlike. The feline italics of her gestures, the liquid flicks of her eyes, the supple grace of her walk. More catlike than the cat even. How you would approach her, tentatively navigating your way across the living room, on ballerina toes, slipping a nervous arm around her waist, scared too bold a gesture might frighten her away. Sometimes she would let you brush her hair while she was watching television. You would comb your fingers through her glossy curls, all the while knowing this was something she was tolerating, just; something she was very much putting up with, her shoulders tense, her cheekbones sharpened into dull, flat flintstones.

Not like the cat who rolled and bloated into your hand at the slightest suggestion of affection.

When she left it came as no surprise, like the ending of a book you'd already read. She just gave up and crawled out.

What is it with women and cats?

He stands up, rubbing his face and slips on his jacket. 'I'd better get going,' he says. 'I have to be up early.' You see him out and he kisses you on the cheek, just once, just on the one cheek. You watch as he shuts the door behind him, noticing he has walked a sycamore leaf into the hall, wrinkled and torn, curled upwards, like an offering palm.

Hank meows from the kitchen. He wants to be fed. You pick him up, staring into the stalagmite limestone of his irises, the charcoal velvet surrounding them; he looks back at you, ribbony and endless, weighted with autopsied understanding.

As Understood By The Women

Jared had not expected to fall in love with a posh girl, it did not fit his plan, but he had, and he was dealing with the situation as best he could.

Elise was posh posh, proper posh, with that posh girl bohemia about her, something he used to find exotic, though now found a little daft, wafting around, thinking herself some idiotic hippy, coral painted toenails and how long she had let her hair grow. There was something very vulgar, very entitled about long hair. He had met her smoking outside his studio, hipbones protruding above her jeans, like sharp little beaks, in a fringed crop top and patent boots. She was sexy in a mean way, in a fuck-you-for-not-understanding-the-vagaries-of-being-very-attractive way. He knew immediately she was somebody he wanted in his life, if only in a minor role, and was pleasantly surprised with each development. His disbelief had crested in this most recent development; her agreement to his proposal of marriage, a proposal that wasn't even romantic or charismatic, a lackadaisical 'How about it?' – over a vongole and a pinot noir, met with a conversely non-committal, 'Sure, why not?' So watery were its foundations, Jared wasn't confident it had actually happened, surprised again when Elise presented him with an ivory padded filofax of ribbon cuttings and seating arrangements. 'Jared,' she said. 'Mummy thinks we should have it in the Spring.'

Since announcing the wedding, Jared had begun sneezing at regular intervals of no more than thirty minutes. It was worst at night and he would often sneeze violently into the early hours of the morning, occasionally sneezing so much he would break down crying; but that did not stop the sneezes. 'Don't be so fucking pathetic,' Elise would say, something she had taken to saying a lot recently, saying it in her posh, sexy way, saying it so liberally the words had lost all meaning.

Jared was an artist, a sculptor, once specialising in giant structures of wood and clay, though now only crafted pieces no bigger than a cat, all of Elise's collarbone. He'd start a project, thinking it to be a swaggering, ambitious structure, work on it for a couple of days, and find he'd just done another collarbone. He surveyed his studio and could see only her collarbone, the jagged, crooked eiderdown of it; its delicate, slicing foliage. He could never admit this preoccupation and on the rare occasions she visited his studio, picking up the collarbones, turning them over in her sepia arms, he would quickly offer, 'This one's about nostalgia; or; this one's about intergenerational poverty in the American South.' She would set them down, disinterestedly, perch on the edge of his workbench and light a cigarette. And he would think of a new way to sculpt her collarbone.

The wedding, it seemed, was understood by the women; like the time he and Elise had gone to dinner with her friend, and she had stared at Elise in a significant way, and they had both risen in silent comprehension, making for the bathroom. 'What was that about?' Jared asked on the way home. 'She needed a tampon,' Elise replied, like he had asked a particularly stupid question. The wedding, he felt, meant nothing to him and something to her, but believed the objective appreciation of this fact meant he would make a Good Husband, and Elise, with all her posh, sexy beauty, deserved at the very least, that.

They met weekly with her parents to plan; he and Elise's father exchanged meaningful eye-rolls beneath meditations on the tonal quality of seat coverings; and in these moments and these moments alone, Jared felt part of some wider confederacy of masculinity, happy at last to have received his invitation. But mostly, he would sneeze and sniff into the handkerchief Elise's mother had given to him; a white handkerchief, naturally.

On the morning of the wedding, he watched guests gather

in the atrium. The sight of so many flowers and fascinators had sent him into a sneezing frenzy, interrupted by one of the bridesmaids, India or Jasmine or some other posh, sexy girl name, hissing, 'She needs to see you. She's in the bathroom.'

'Knock knock,' he ventured, tapping at the door. 'Isn't it bad luck for the groom to see the bride before the wedding?'

'Don't be so fucking pathetic,' Elise called back, and he stepped in, sniffling. Elise was fussing with her hair in the mirror. 'Is everything okay?' he asked. 'Can you get me a drink?' she replied, hoisting up her dress, pulling down her knickers and then sitting on the toilet. 'Can you get me an old fashioned?' she said, surprising him, always. She tore off two squares of toilet tissue and navigated them beneath the ruffles of lace.

He could see now the marriage would not last. He didn't understand her, and he hadn't even tried to; like asking a person with hands for feet why they can't dance with you, instead of asking why they have hands for feet. He thought she looked beautiful, not in a posh way, not in a sexy way, just properly, classically beautiful. Her wide, slender collarbone had never looked better, her luminous skin pulled taut across it, sinking hypnotically into the geometric perfection of her clavicle. She stood up, flushed the toilet and turned to face him, rubbing her lips together; plump, pouty lips, that seemed everyone's to kiss, but in this moment, in this bathroom, were his and only his; like water trickling pleasantly through your fingers.

'I love you,' he said. 'And I truly believe I will love you forever.'

'Don't be so fucking pathetic,' Elise replied, taking a tissue and wiping his nose.

Tributaries

As the tears and Tanqueray passed, the listens to *Blood On The Tracks* less frequent, the horizon staggered into sight, the world stuttered statements of promise again. 'C'mon!' Melody found herself exclaiming to her friends, palms heavenward, arms held crooked at her side. 'C'mon!' She had not factored this infant joie-de-vivre, her beautiful, bouncing baby, would not be shared by her pals, who had not suffered the recent blow of heartbreak, the rapturous recovery from which, knitting over only the tiny gaps, the 'I saw him on Facebook, talking to his ex-girlfriend!', the 'He doesn't care whether we repaint the kitchen green or lime green! He doesn't care at all.' She felt like a paraplegic, sensing twinges in her legs – she wanted to go dancing! – but this didn't fit into the neatly folded tapestry of her social circle's lives. They had partners and meetings. Kitchens to repaint in lime green. What a life. What an old ballbag of a thing. And so, she went alone, woozy off the audacity of it, the way you feel in the first flushes of autumn. At first, nervous ventures, the occasional gingerbread latte in Starbucks on the way home from work, graduating to trips to the cinema, folding her coat on one seat, placing her bag on the other, chewing fistfuls of popcorn, half salty half sweet, mining kernels from her teeth in the dark. Manchester, the city she had grown up in, felt like an old friend.

Josie cancelled their dinner in favour of a spinning class, a cavalier move she was prone to; and Melody went alone, ordering a steak sandwich and a Jayne Mansfield, meat and liquor, sitting at the bar. She surveyed her surroundings, hopeless vignettes sellotaped to their surroundings; the dreadful taxonomy of it; boxing off into would and wouldn't. It was a hamper of age, being single alone. In her early twenties she had a large group of single girlfriends, dolled up and out, terrifying in their industry and numbers; though in her mid-thirties found her friends were only occasionally alone, their heads popping singularly above the parapet, like Whac-A-Moles. She plucked a pound coin from her purse, slipping it into the jukebox, selecting *I Can't Stand The Rain*, anticipating the tipsy, Tejano intro, hearing instead the slicing vocal fry, the rippling melancholy of *Blue*. She'd messed up the selection, why did she always do that? She returned to her sandwich, eating with her hands, dabbing blood from her lips. She noticed a man at the other side of the bar; attractive, but roughly so. He looked like a painting with a schlocky title, The Artist Arrives; or Untitled (The Artist Arrives). He was not the kind she readily identified as Her Type; he was too unmade, too unfinished, but found she had started to like that; attraction you had to work for, that you had to earn. She was done, she thought, chasing beauty. It was for sad, lonely people, chasing beauty. She at last understood its secrets, and true to form, its charms were fleeting. She sipped her cocktail wishing she could affect the heavy lidded, ham-fisted sex appeal of some women. Women who just put it out there. Women who didn't deal in tricks and winks; stealing glances of him from across the bar, smiles dispatched like roofies. He finished his drink and left his seat, approaching her, placing his hat on the bar top next to her and ordered a drink.

'I thought your hat had a feather in it,' she said, staring straight ahead. These things, she found, were better delivered with little if any post-analysis. She glanced at the hat, thinking if she considered herself cute, she might put it on.

'Nope,' he replied. 'No feather.' She cocked her head and finished her cocktail.

'I could have sworn it had a feather in it,' she repeated, taking a bite of her sandwich. He looked at her, amused.

'Can I get you a drink?' he asked, and she told him yes he could.

She met her friends for lunch. 'I met someone,' she told them. 'I met a Canadian.'

His name was Todd and he was from Ontario, which made him seem a little bit exotic and a little bit approachable. Josie picked up a bread roll letting the rolled oats fall through her fingers. 'What does he do?' she asked. It was the peculiar sort of question her friends had taken to asking lately; this strange assessment of estate and cache, this sizing up of value. What does anyone ever really do? I mean, really?

Josie had gotten married in the Spring. 'I thought you were against marriage?' Melody had asked. 'Oh sure, I'm against it,' she replied. 'Oh sure, I'm still against it.' Integrity, Melody had found, seemed less important as they grew older; a show pony quality, all meat and no potatoes. 'I'm happy for you,' she had said, but the word had stuck in her throat like something on loan; anyway, the hell kind of a word was happy? Lucy signalled over to the waiter, who was approaching with their drinks. She knocked back a gin fizz, her cheeks flushing crimson. She had started seeing a carpenter. 'A carpenter!' she cried. 'Jesus Mary Joseph!' She liked to cook the girls dinner on a Thursday. She made them a risotto then ushered them into the kitchen, revealing a glossy mahogany spice rack. 'He made me this,' she whispered. 'He made me this and I didn't even ask for it.' She thought about Todd, about having the thing, the thing you didn't even ask for. She liked him, she thought, she liked how he looked at her; the earthy, earnest look of a man raised on syrups and smiles, on chicory and fiction, with the crisp crunch of snow underfoot and the mountains and sky on high. How when she had told him she was from Levenshulme, he'd repeated 'Lebensraum?' How she had wondered how early one should invoke the Third Reich in a relationship. Whether you should just get it over with right from the start.

They ordered more cocktails; vodka and cranberry, a generational thing, like peace signs in polaroids, culottes.

Melody felt suddenly giddy, and grabbed their hands across the table, squeezing in a jejune benediction. 'Us girls!' she exclaimed. 'Us girls!'

It started snowing. 'I love the snow,' Todd said, rolling onto his back. 'It's my favourite part of living in Canada.'

She turned to face him, resting her head on his shoulder.

'I love the snow too,' she said. 'It's like bits of the universe falling down on you. It's like kisses from the cosmos.'

He stared at her softly, stroking her chin; the way men did when you said something whimsical.

'I need a shower,' he said, huffing himself up and out of bed, kissing her on the way.

She watched him close the bathroom door. It was nice to have someone again. It had been a little over a year since she had split up with her ex-boyfriend, and he felt so completely, so irredeemably, removed.

He started seeing someone just weeks after they split. 'He's just afraid of being alone!' her friends had cooed but it was not to be sneered at. Everyone wanted a sweetheart. Love was sneaky like that. It found a warm nook, a safe space, and crept in, settling there like an unwelcome houseguest; and suddenly you couldn't go about your business, walk around in your pyjamas, without a flush of embarrassment, a blushing, biting knowing. Todd emerged from the shower, shrouded by steam, wrapped in a long, brown bath towel. There was something sturdy about him. He sat next to her on the bed, the soft fold of his stomach pouting over the bath towel like a sullen bottom lip. She studied the side of his jaw. The poppyseed polkadot of his freshly shaved face. He curled his hand around her ear, sending a shiver of pleasure down her spine. She held his face and looked into his eyes. She had never really looked into someone's eyes and gotten all the way in before. There was always some roadblock, and she'd stumble back on herself, embarrassed to be caught out so far. She wondered how open she was, how much she let in, imagining herself some airy barn, some spirited Bring & Buy, come one come all. Hopelessly, resentfully, she felt she might be falling in love. The nervous high of love. The sick-making knowledge of it. She punched him on the arm. The swirling perfection of the thing! The feathers and jazz of the thing! But when the curtains came down and the showgirls removed their suits; what was left bar the foot rubs and the flowers? I mean, where do you go from there?

He came to see her at work.

She owned a shop in South Manchester. Flowers In The Attic. 'I don't arrange flowers,' she'd say. 'I curate them.' It had started snowing again and she asked Jo, her assistant, to take the display arrangements inside. Snow was bad news for flowers. Snow was bad news for a lot of things. Jo was a History student; making sense of stuff that happened, a discipline Melody could get on board with. He was gay; but didn't think he had realised yet. She felt a little guilty in the knowing, like she had seen journal entries he hadn't yet written, and would drop little hints, telling turns of phrase, 'I believe you're of the historical persuasion!'; or, 'I wouldn't Bette Midler on it!' believing these nuanced suggestions served to usher him along the path to enlightenment. She could be pretty nice like that.

She watched Todd wander about the shop, picking up the arrangements, commenting on their comeliness. He looked so ragged and out of place, his thick khaki jacket and heavy boots moving amongst the petals. The worm in the bud, alright. Get the hell out of here! – she thought, but to her credit, did not say. 'You know, this place reminds me of somewhere back home,' Todd said, and Melody felt suddenly annoyed; watching him swagger amongst the gladioli, manhandle the petunias. Why do things always have to be like something else? she thought. Why can't they themselves be the thing?

A couple came in. Melody had this strange habit of staring

at couples, unable to believe they even existed at all. She liked it when couples came in to pick out flowers together. Last week she had sold a lavish bouquet to a young man for his girlfriend's birthday. 'We're total soulmates,' he'd said, though it seemed the sort of statement that should be delivered only as a duet; speak for yourself, why don't you? She helped them sort through some funeral arrangements; her livelihood depended on ceremony, on the punctuations of rites of passage; falling in love and dying.

They had dinner at Todd's, drowsy on red wine, propped up by pillows. Todd flicked through the channels while Melody stared into space; happy in sleepy silence. They settled on a film about a boy with a growth on his face, who woke up one day without a growth on his face. He got made captain of the football team, prom king and valedictorian. He got invited to the best parties at the fanciest houses and had sex with all the prettiest girls. Everyone loved him. But gradually the growth grew back and he became fond of it, realising everyone had only ever loved him when he didn't have a growth on his face. He called the growth Kevin and sang *You Are The Sunshine Of My Life* to it in the mirror every morning. The film ended with him shaving, nicking the growth with a razor, slicing it off, and it wouldn't grow back. It was an ambiguous finale but basically you understood that the boy had killed himself. Melody thought it was a pretty funny movie. Todd reached over and stroked her hair. She curled into him like a cat.

'Can I ask you something?' Todd asked softly.

'Anything,' Melody replied, burrowing her face beneath his arm.

'Can I pee on you?'

A few weeks after Melody had split up with her ex-boyfriend some guy buzzed up to the flat knocking on her front door looking for his friend. Melody had leaned against the door frame; she had spent most of the day crying, feeling limpid and drooped, like everything had been sucked out of her. She wore grey sweats and a thinned white t-shirt, and her hair was scraped back into a high ponytail. She blinked wearily at him, said his friend must live on a different floor. He asked if he could maybe just hang out with her for a bit, and with a twitch of her shoulder she invited him in, and they'd had sex. She thought about the incident daily. She thought about how she was a person capable of doing that, if that was maybe apparent when looking at her. She lifted her head from Todd's shoulder. She wondered how much time she could let lapse before answering the question.

'We don't really say pee here,' she replied. 'Piss. Wee. Urinate. But not pee.' She tapped his arm with her finger. Todd wriggled out from beneath her, standing over the settee. He seemed suddenly boyish and lost.

'I didn't realise,' he said, searching the room, his face creasing. 'I'm going to make a cup of tea,' he said. 'Do you want a cup of tea?'

She lay back into the couch as he walked into the kitchen, stretching out, pushing her toes into the arms, enjoying the freedom of the space. She wondered if this was what sex essentially was. Presenting ourselves at our most horrible and wanting still to be accepted. That we wanted more from it than what it essentially was. She had done this before; handing a stranger her big dopey heart. She thought about how things ended last time. There had been cracks, sure, the frosty silences, the late nights, but it wasn't until he announced he was taking singing lessons that she fully understood how deep they ran. Oh, she knew she had been stifling him, holy hell, she knew full well. But... singing lessons! The thought! Well, let him sing, she'd said. Let him intone his heart's song, whatever that might be. But then he announced he was leaving her for his singing teacher, an older woman with beautifully preserved hands.

Todd returned with two cups of tea. He looked like he was

poised to make some grand, romantic gesture, running across the room, sweeping her into his arms, but considering the practicalities, the setting down of the tea, the waxy slip of the hardwood floor, thought better of it, instead winking and half-turning his face; what's cooking good looking?

'I'm going to bed,' he said. 'Are you coming?'

It was silly, she thought. All this squeezing onto one raft when two would do.

'I'll just pee a minute,' she replied.

'What?'

'I'll just be a minute,' she said.

She switched off the television, thinking about the boy with the growth on his face, half wishing she had some terrible physical deformity she could sing to, a reason never to leave the flat.

They went to the countryside at Todd's insistence. He was getting fed up of the city, he'd said and so they drove out to Cheshire, to the countryside, the fields clotted with lumps of snow; the leafy idylls and pastoral pastures sweeping past in mopey greys and greens. They passed a cemetery. It looked strange blanketed in white. Animated, really. The headstones peeping up like erect postage stamps, stone crosses like limbs burst through the ice. It was good to drive past a cemetery. It could give a day a sense of gravity.

'There's no Pret,' Melody said stepping out of the car. 'There's no Starbucks. What the hell are we doing here?' She felt vulnerable and unmade; when sleep still lingers dimensionally around you. She yawned. Todd was wearing, she noticed, the same hat he wore when they first met. She hadn't seen him wear it since, and was happy of this small, shared history.

'Ok,' he said. 'Let's go.'

The walk was beautiful, damp and cold; the snow adding an additional eeriness; the crackling sludge, black twigs piercing the icy white; it looked extra-terrestrial. They walked through the fields and farms, stopping to pet horses; dabbing the flat hair of their necks. They climbed the hills. Todd helped Melody bumble over stiles, pulling her away from puddles. They seemed to have regressed to a more chivalrous time; returning to a natural rural order. They reached one of the snowy peaks, leaning against the fence, looking out over the view.

'This is a view,' Todd said. 'Now this is a view.' Melody looked at him, wanting to fix him in the moment, to screenshot him, to figure him out.

'I hate Manchester,' he said, pushing himself from the fence. 'I gotta tell you. I can't stand Manchester.' He turned and walked back downhill.

On the way down they followed the meandering lines of a river, the water moving sluggishly, iced in the snow. It was nice to have a line to follow. It was like colouring in. 'I wonder what river this is,' Melody said. 'It's not a river,' Todd replied. 'It's a tributary.' Melody studied the water; it looked pretty wide, commanding. It looked like something you could drown in.

'What's the difference?' she asked.

'Tributaries don't flow into the ocean,' Todd replied. 'They're not the main stem. They're more like the drainage system. They're just the little things that make up the whole.'

Melody followed the rippling waves of the stream with her eyes, the water bubbling up and over the rocks, carrying with it twigs and leaves. How could one spot the difference? How could one know whether or not it was the main affair, the definite article.

'I dunno,' Todd said, looking at her, and then the stream, flippantly. 'You just know.'

Todd dropped Melody off at the tram station. He rested his hat on the dashboard and she picked it up and put it on her head. She turned to Todd and smiled. He swiped it from her head and placed it back in front of the wheel. A feather fell in her palm, ragged and bitten, too old and crumpled to float. 'Look!' she said. 'Look! – It did have a feather in it!'

'Your hat!' she said. 'Remember when I first met you, you said it didn't; but it did. It must have been tucked into the lapel or something.' She let it go and it twirled, sort of, falling onto his knee. He wiped it off and it landed beneath his feet on the car floor. Todd parked in front of the tram stop, turning off the engine. You were lots of little things. You were the deflection until you were the one. And even if you were, it hardly made any difference, you still found yourself crying into your pea soup, swirling it around, sniffling. She sat quite comfortably in the car seat, her clothes damp and sticky, her shirt clinging to her back. She spent her life, she realised, impassively content and yet unable to settle. Like being full and hungry at the same time. She could graze forever.

'I have a wife,' Todd said, turning to her. 'In Canada.'

Melody blinked.

'Come on,' he said. 'You knew.' She did. She did know. Of course she did. She stared out at the windscreen. She was already gone. She was already outta there!

'Do you hate me?' he asked, caring; but also, not caring at all. She watched his mouth move, imagining the squinting twang of his accent, and thought she'd always thought he'd sounded stupid, like he was putting it on. It started snowing again and she got out the car and stood at his window. He rolled it down.

'It was nice knowing you,' she said, kissing his cheek. And it was.

She sat quietly on the tram, not listening to music, not reading, just watching the countryside slowly populate with life. She hopped off the tram at Deansgate, the snow falling lightly, whipped up by the breeze, swirling in a peculiar migratory pattern. She turned onto Whitworth Street, the cold delicious and tingling, like someone blowing on your neck. The red brick buildings were tall and warm against the dark; the snow, like dancing pieces of stray fluff, floating hypnotically around them. How could he hate this city? How could anyone? She walked down Oxford Road, the busiest bus route in Europe, as everyone seemed so keen to espouse, a street he had walked down, her friends had walked down, her family had walked down. She thought how lucky she was to have loved so many people all contained within one place, how any one of them, as unique and arbitrary as the snow, could step outside their house and feel it fall coolly on their face; how weird and beautiful it was that they were, in this way, connected.

Acknowledgements

Thanks to Adrian for taking a chance on the collection.
Thanks to Robbie, Laura and all the people at Freight for
doing such a great job with it and being completely excellent
all round

Thanks to Becky, a real pal and to Rodge for being an
amazing (patient) editor.

Thanks to Nick and the Manchester Writing School.

Thanks to Suzanne Barron, Cristina Delgado, Eddie Harris,
Victoria Hutton, Frances Walker(s), Roz Webster, Emily
Wykes and all of the Pins. Thanks to Alex my kin, Claire my
first love, Charlotte my darling girl. To Matthew for a giant
heart, Clare for unbridled support and inspiration, Amanda
for knocking me off my feet. Thank you Peet for all things.

And to all my other brilliant friends, friends of friends, and
everyone else who has helped. I love and appreciate you very
much.

Finally, thanks to my family for absolutely everything.

Credits

It Begins first appeared on Litro
A Lover's Guide To Meeting Shy Girls; Or; Break Up Record
first appeared on Metazen
The Small Written Thing appeared as a Little Fiction title
Dates first appeared on The Pygmy Giant
Taxidermy first appeared in The Lighthouse Journal
A Single Lady's Manual for Parent/Teacher Evening first
appeared on McSweeney's Internet Tendency
The Getting Of the Cat first appeared on Blank Media
As Understood By The Women first appeared in Unthology 8